=2      26

50

WITHDRAWN

Echoes of Massacre Canyon

ECHOES OF
MASSACRE CANYON

BEN TYLER

FIVE STAR

A part of Gale, Cengage Learning

GALE
CENGAGE Learning·

Farmington Hills, Mich • San Francisco • New York • Waterville, Maine
Meriden, Conn • Mason, Ohio • Chicago

LIBRARY OF CONGRESS CATALOGING-IN-PUBLICATION DATA

Names: Tyler, Ben, author.
Title: Echoes of Massacre Canyon / Ben Tyler.
Description: First edition. | Waterville, Maine : Five Star, a part of Gale, Cengage Learning, [2016]
Identifiers: LCCN 2015038002| ISBN 9781432831387 (hardcover) | ISBN 1432831380 (hardcover) | ISBN 9781432831509 (ebook) | ISBN 143283150x (ebook)
Subjects: | BISAC: FICTION / Historical. | FICTION / Westerns. | GSAFD: Western stories. | Adventure fiction.
Classification: LCC PS3620.Y58 E29 2016 | DDC 813/.6—dc23
LC record available at http://lccn.loc.gov/2015038002

First Edition. First Printing: March 2016
Find us on Facebook– https://www.facebook.com/FiveStarCengage
Visit our website– http://www.gale.cengage.com/fivestar/
Contact Five Star™ Publishing at FiveStar@cengage.com

Printed in the United States of America
1 2 3 4 5 6 7 20 19 18 17 16

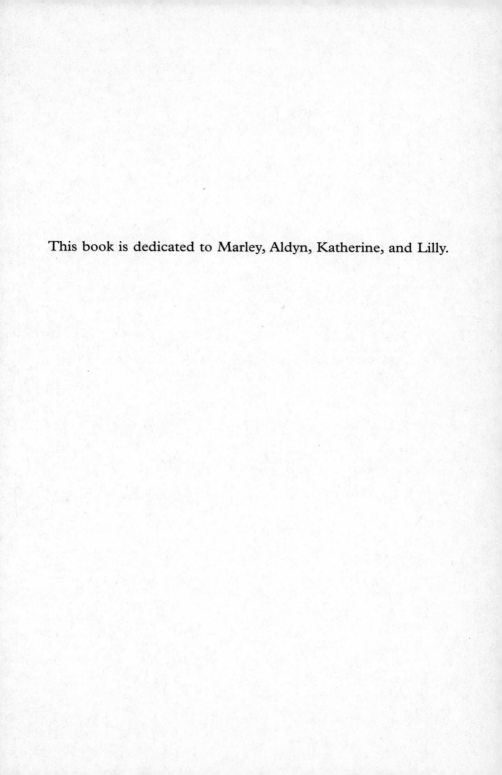

This book is dedicated to Marley, Aldyn, Katherine, and Lilly.

PROLOGUE:
SOUTHWEST TEXAS,
LATE SUMMER, 1869

Corporal Clint Ramsay squatted on his heels and studied the sandy, rocky soil in front of him. He passed his hand lightly over the hoofprints, then sifted a handful of gritty sand through his fingers. He stood and wiped his hands on his blue trousers. Ramsay took a deep breath as he stared at the distant sun-tinted mesas and hills with their maze of narrow, steep-walled canyons.

He didn't like what he was thinking.

Lieutenant Elias McKendrick rode up behind Ramsay. "Well, Corporal?"

Ramsay pointed toward the rugged terrain to the west. "They're two hours ahead, maybe three at the most. But they're headed straight into territory we might want to avoid."

"Territory we might want to avoid?" McKendrick asked. "We've been chasing that bunch of renegade Comanches for a day and a half. I don't see any reason to stop chasing them now. We've gained considerable ground on them."

Ramsay looked back at the fifteen troopers of the Third US Cavalry who had been on the trail of the Comanche party ever since their escape from Fort Simpson. The troopers were bone weary and saddle sore. And, if asked, they would likely say they were anxious about what might lie ahead just over the next ridge.

The tall, lanky corporal took a step toward his young commanding officer and said, "Lieutenant, this band of Quohadi

Comanches is led by a warrior named Wolf Eye. You're new to the territory, and I know that name doesn't mean anything to you. But if you keep after him, and follow him into his own homeland where he knows every rock, tree, and rattlesnake on a personal basis, you might live to regret it—if you live at all."

"That's enough, Corporal!"

Ramsay knew he was dancing close to the edge of a dangerous precipice with the officer and was bordering on insubordination. But to remain quiet and let the young officer, who was fresh out of West Point, lead the detachment into one of Wolf Eye's traps was unthinkable.

"And one more thing, Lieutenant. You're of the opinion that you're *chasing* the Comanches. I can tell you, with some certainty, that you're not chasing the Comanches—they're *leading* you."

McKendrick stiffened in his saddle. "How dare you!" The young lieutenant glared at him and was about to respond when a rider came charging over a rise toward them at a gallop.

Civilian scout Harley Fry skidded his horse to a stop in front of the two men and pointed back in the direction from which he'd come. "I found two more dead horses over amongst a clump of mesquite a while back," he said. "That makes five. They'll either have to find fresh mounts, or scatter on foot."

"Give me your opinion, Fry," McKendrick said. He jerked a thumb over at Ramsay. "Corporal Ramsay has already given me his."

Fry shot a spray of tobacco juice at a lizard and said, "I figure Wolf Eye is countin' on us to follow him into one of those canyons where he aims to get our horses. And fer him to get our horses, he's gotta get us first. He's lettin' us get closer to him on purpose, Lieutenant. You'd better be cautious from here on out."

McKendrick looked from Fry to Ramsay, then said, "We will

continue going forward, gentlemen. I believe you are giving far too much credit to this ignorant savage. You would have me believe he is Napoleon, George Washington, and U. S. Grant all rolled into one."

"Best not to underestimate him, Lieutenant," Fry said.

McKendrick nudged his horse back toward the column. "Corporal Ramsay, return to the column and get in line. Fry, you keep me informed of what you find."

Ramsay returned to the detachment and squeezed his horse in beside Corporal Ed Wilhoit.

"The lieutenant didn't like your opinion, huh?" Wilhoit asked.

"Nope. But I expected worse from him. And unless I miss my guess, things are about to get worse for all of us."

Half an hour later, the column approached the mouth of a narrow, high-walled canyon. Ramsay knew of the canyon; he and Fry had been through it twice on patrols in years past. It wasn't a place to be riding into with Wolf Eye and his followers somewhere ahead of them.

Ramsay then saw Fry waving his arms over his head and shouting.

Lieutenant McKendrick halted the column and turned in his saddle. "Corporal Ramsay. To the front, on the double."

"Be cautious," Wilhoit said, as Ramsay rode away to join McKendrick and Fry.

Fry pointed toward the canyon. "Wolf Eye found hisself some horses, Lieutenant. And a passel of rifles and ammunition along with them."

"Damn," McKendrick said.

"Tracks show they've vamoosed. I reckon they're headed to the Rio Grande country now."

McKendrick motioned the column forward. They rode into the canyon where remnants of what had once been a mule pack train were scattered along the canyon floor. Burning wagons, smashed crates, dead mules and horses—and bloody, mutilated bodies.

The heat was lying low and shimmering off the oven-like rocks within the walls of the canyon. It was quick to do its work on the dead. Ramsay pulled his bandanna from his neck and tied it around his nose and mouth. The other troopers soon followed suit. The tails of their horses began flitting back and forth as a cloud of flies attacked everything in sight. Black long-necked vultures picked at the bloodied mule and horse carcasses, while giving little ground to the approaching riders.

"Never seed so much blood," Fry said. "And I've been in some bad skirmishes."

Ramsay watched as Lieutenant McKendrick jumped off his horse and began retching. Behind him, he could hear a couple of troopers doing likewise. He wasn't so sure he could hold it in either.

Ramsay rode past a dozen or more scalped and mutilated men lying among the scattered debris. *Mexican banditos.* They were being picked at by the buzzards. He took off his hat and slapped it hard against his leg. "Get outta here, you black bastards!"

There was a loud whooshing sound as the startled birds took flight, but they landed undeterred moments later a few yards away to continue their feed on a dead mule.

"We were so close," McKendrick said, as he wiped his mouth with a handkerchief and remounted.

"I reckon you're right," Fry said. "But we coulda blundered into this trap just like these Mexicans did. Only they done us a big favor and got here first." Fry waved his hand at the bloody carnage. "Take a good look around and remember what yur seeing, Lieutenant. This is what Wolf Eye had in mind fer us."

McKendrick turned and rode away.

Ramsay and Fry dismounted and walked among the bodies and the strewn items, looking for anything to provide identification of the dead.

"Not much left," Fry said.

"It looks as though these *banditos* had been raiding the settlements to the north and had their wagons and mules loaded with plunder. They never had a chance once the Comanches caught 'em in this canyon."

"Best to be cautious in Comanche territory. I 'spect the young lieutenant learned a good lesson here today."

Ramsay walked over to the edge of the canyon walls where there was a flat rocky outcropping. As he approached the outcropping, he heard a noise coming from behind the rock. He pulled his revolver as a precaution against the unknown. He crouched low and circled around behind the rock, wary of what, or who, he might find there. When he reached the back of the outcropping, he was astounded at what he found.

"Well, I'll be a—"

Standing in front of him was a little girl wearing a tattered blue dress that fit tight around her neck, and reached down past her ankles. She appeared to be around eight or nine years old with dirty trails on her cheeks where tears had once flowed. Her blue eyes were now dry, but they were wide with fear. She was on the thin side, and had brownish-blonde hair that hung down past her shoulders in long strands.

Ramsay was not sure what to do, but he knew he had to do something. And he had to do it now. The little girl was frightened and needed to know that she was safe. He reached out his arms and beckoned to her: "You're safe now, sweetheart. We're not going to hurt you."

She hesitated for a moment then looked over her shoulder and cried out, "Elizano! Elizano!" She turned and ran back toward the rocks.

Ramsay ran after her and caught her by the arm. "Wait, wait. Don't run. I'm not going to hurt you."

She kicked him, and beat at him with her small, balled-up fists, then collapsed to the ground.

Ramsay let go of her arm and knelt down beside her. "Easy, now. I'll not let anyone hurt you. You're safe now, I promise. I'll not let anything happen to you."

Tears began streaming down her face as she leaped into his waiting arms and buried her face on his shoulder.

Her body shook as Ramsay whispered to her, "You're safe now, sweetheart, you're safe now."

McKendrick joined him when he became aware of the little girl. He laid a hand on Ramsay's shoulder as he stared at her and said, "Corporal, I had expected a few surprises on this mission, but this sure wasn't one of them."

"Take a good look around, Lieutenant. This is more than a surprise; this is nothing less than a miracle."

McKendrick nodded his head. "Yes, you are right. Well, she seems to be comfortable with you, so take her over to where the horses are being held and get her away from all this carnage. I'll hurry the men along and we'll be gone from this place before dark."

Corporal Clint Ramsay, with the little blue-eyed girl's head still buried on his shoulder, walked over to the horses. There they sat huddled together in silence while the troopers finished their gory tasks.

High above them, a lone Mexican man looked down on them unseen from behind a brush-covered ledge. A small smile creased his lips as he watched a soldier carry the little girl away from the rocks where he had left her. He then returned to the work he had begun.

CHAPTER ONE:
TWELVE YEARS LATER—1881

Clint Ramsay walked down the stairs of the Heritage Hotel in Kansas City, Missouri, with the morning *Kansas City Times* tucked under his arm. He strolled across the elegant brass-filled lobby and plopped down in a plush green velveteen chair that was his usual morning headquarters when he was in town.

He scanned the lobby as he always did before opening the newspaper. The first person he noticed was a large Englishman in a tweed jacket, sporting a thick red beard. The stranger was surrounded by six pieces of luggage and three leather gun cases. Alongside the Englishman stood a beautiful dark-haired woman who appeared to be several years younger than the man. She was dressed in a tan ankle-length hunting outfit and a colorful broad-brimmed sombrero. She was smiling and holding on to the Englishman's every word.

Ramsay had always been amazed at the variety of guests—and their garb—that passed through the hotel's lobby. To him, observing the guests of the hotel was better entertainment than attending a performance of Valentine Rogers over at the music hall.

Albert, the dapper little hotel concierge, came over to him with a steaming cup of coffee, which he placed on a small round table at Ramsay's elbow. "Good morning, Mister Ramsay. Black with one sugar, just as you like it."

"Morning, Albert. And thanks for the coffee." Clint ducked

his head toward the Englishman and asked, "A big wig from England?"

"The Duke of Willingham and his bride. They're on their honeymoon."

"Looks like the duke made a good choice if his bride agreed to go on a hunting trip for her honeymoon. I'd say that's a little out of the ordinary, even for the English."

Albert looked all around the lobby, then leaned over and whispered, "Between the two of us, I can tell you that the honeymoon thing is the duke's private joke. The woman's real name is Ruby Ridgeway. The duke found her in a Saint Louis bar and brought her along for his personal entertainment. She's being well compensated for her part in this hunting trip."

Ramsay laughed. "Well, what good is it to be rich if you can't flaunt it?"

Albert returned to his work at the desk and left Clint alone with his coffee and newspaper. Clint scanned the printed page looking for anything that might pique his interest. President Garfield had been shot a few days earlier, so that was old news. So was the article lauding Pat Garrett for his valor in bringing Billy Bonney to justice. He had known Garrett back in the days when the sheriff was a bartender and was skeptical of all the praise that was being heaped in his direction. Another familiar name grabbed his attention: Sitting Bull. The old Dakota Sioux chief had held out as long as he could and surrendered to the federal troops up north at Fort Buford.

He had finished reading about Sitting Bull, when he sensed someone standing in front of him. He lowered the paper and peered over the top. A short, thin man with a weather-beaten face looked down at him. The man wore a greasy buckskin shirt with long fringes hanging from the sleeves and gray, threadbare corduroy pants. A single braid of gray hair hung down his back past his shoulders. His left jaw poked out from a thick chaw of tobacco.

Clint folded the newspaper and dropped it in the chair next to him. "Morning, Harley."

"Morning," Harley Fry said, as he lowered himself on his haunches in front of Clint. "You look mighty pert this morning. You goin' to a tea party?"

Clint put his thumbs under the lapels of his blue corduroy jacket and flipped them. "Might, if one happens to come along."

Clint then heard a commotion at the front of the lobby and turned to take a look. The Englishman and his young companion were walking arm in arm out the front door, followed by a procession of servants who were straining under the weight of their luggage.

"That duke might invite me to one of his parties. You always preached at me to be prepared for any contingency."

"I think it was war parties I was referrin' to, not tea parties."

Clint grinned at his old friend and asked, "What brings you out this way, or do I want to know?"

"Lucas wants to see you."

"Any idea what he wants?"

"Nope, he didn't say."

Clint and Harley went back a long way; back to their years riding with the US cavalry. Harley's age was anyone's guess and he wasn't telling. Clint knew that Harley was several decades older than his own thirty-one years, and was about half a foot shorter than his own six feet three inches. Still, the old scout had the resolve and tenacity of a much younger man. Even though they were a pair mismatched by age, appearance, and experience, the two men had ridden together, and had watched out for each other for more than sixteen years.

"I brung your horse along. We'll be out front when you're ready to git."

Clint stood and stretched his arms over his head. His left shoulder still ached from the bullet wound he had received in Colorado, but it was beginning to loosen up some.

"I'll be along in a few minutes. I expect I ought to go change clothes and gather up my gear. Lucas might want us on the move again."

Half an hour later, Clint dismounted in front of the four-story Blaylock Building. The top two floors of the limestone office building were the home of the Underwood Detective Agency. From behind his saddle, he removed a leather satchel that held the tools of his trade: a Colt .45-caliber handgun with well-worn black-walnut grips, a leather gun belt with holster attached, two changes of denims, socks, underwear, and shirts.

Clint entered the front door, climbed two sets of stairs, and headed for Lucas Underwood's office. The door to the office was closed, but Clint opened it and walked in unannounced.

Lucas sat behind an ancient, scarred oak desk with his head buried in a stack of papers. He was a heavyset man with graying hair and wore wire-rimmed eyeglasses. A giant cigar hung from the side of his mouth. He was so engrossed in his work that he failed to notice he had a visitor.

Clint cleared his throat.

Lucas looked up from his desk and removed his eyeglasses. He leaned back in his swivel chair, took the cigar from his mouth, and said, "You've been loafing long enough. It's high time you got back in harness."

"Well, good morning to you, too. Yes, sir, I've had a grand morning. Thank you for asking."

"Cut the buffalo dung and take a seat," Lucas said. "How's the shoulder?"

Clint placed his right hand on his injured left shoulder and massaged it. "It's not quite like new yet. I was lucky that the bullet ricocheted off a rock and took most of the blow before it hit me. The doctor told me to keep moving it so it wouldn't bind up. It should recover to full use in a few days."

Lucas shook the ashes off his cigar and said, "This ain't an easy business we're in, is it?"

"No, sir, it's not," Clint replied. "Not easy at all. Nor is it favorable for living a long and happy life."

"You've been with me . . . what . . . three years?"

"It was three years in May."

"I've never asked, but how does this detective work compare to your eight years with the Texas Rangers?"

Clint grinned. "Well, you haven't sent me out to bring in any Comanche or Kiowa raiding parties yet." His face then turned serious as he added, "There's a lot of turmoil these days, Lucas. There are countless out-of-work soldiers roaming the countryside who are angry, disillusioned, and plain old hungry. They've faced death and now they're on the prowl to get what they can, any way they can: banks, railroads, freight outfits. They're a dangerous breed."

Lucas nodded his head. "I know. We've rounded up our share of them, but it seems to be a bottomless pit."

"And a profitable pit for you," Clint said.

Lucas was the founder, owner, and chief honcho of the Underwood Detective Agency. Lucas had gotten his start with the Scotsman, Allan Pinkerton, from whom he had learned the investigation trade from the bottom rung of the ladder up. During the recent war, Lucas had taken on several spy assignments for Pinkerton. Some were routine, some were dangerous. A few meant crossing battle lines to bring back information the higher-ups deemed critical to the Union's battle strategy.

After the war, Lucas left the Pinkertons and traveled west, along with the steady flow of immigrants who were seeking a better life. He settled in Kansas City and opened his own detective agency at the behest of several wealthy mine owners and ranchers.

Lucas's eyes narrowed as he studied Clint. "That was good work out in Colorado. The mine owner was well pleased that you and Hooper rounded up those high-graders as quick as you did."

"We got a break when a scorned lover decided to get revenge on one of the outlaws. She named names and gave away their hideout. The rest was easy."

Lucas searched through his papers and retrieved a telegram. "Do you know a man named . . . let's see . . . Wilhoit? Ed Wilhoit?"

"Ed Wilhoit? Now that's a name I haven't heard spoken in years." He leaned forward in his chair and stared at his boss, curious why he was now hearing a name from his past. "Yes, I know Ed Wilhoit. I once rode with him back when I was with the cavalry. Why are you asking?"

Lucas handed the telegram across the desk. "This came to the office, but it's addressed to you. I thought it might mean something to you."

Clint looked at the telegram.

To Clint Ramsay:
I need you in San Reale, Texas.
You are involved. Hurry.

Sheriff Ed Wilhoit.

He looked up at Lucas. "Ed and I were never what you would call close friends. He was a good man, but hard to get to know. We rode together for a couple of years before I moved on to the Texas Rangers. I never knew what happened to him."

"Looks like he remembered you."

Clint figured that Ed would be around fifty years old now, give or take. He was a no-nonsense man through and through.

He'd never backed away from anyone or anything. If it was in front of him, he went through it, not around it. And he was not a man given to asking for help.

It was the telegram's final line that troubled Ramsay: *You are involved. Hurry.*

Clint folded the telegram and put it in his shirt pocket. He stood and turned toward the door. "I'll be back in a couple of weeks, Lucas. I've got to go to Texas and see what this is all about."

"I thought so," Lucas said. "Let Oliver make all the arrangements for you. And take that old reprobate Fry with you. I'll cover the expenses as a bonus for your work in Colorado."

"Well, aren't you the generous one."

Lucas stuck the cigar back in his mouth and returned to his paperwork. "But don't dawdle around in Texas renewing old acquaintances. Get on back here and earn your pay, you hear? My generosity only goes so far."

CHAPTER TWO

Clint went to his office and sat with his feet spread out on his desk, his hands clasped behind his head. The mystery of the telegram intrigued him. All he could think of was that it had to be a serious matter or Ed Wilhoit would never have asked for help. That was out of character for the man he remembered. He dropped his feet to the floor and rummaged through his desk, searching for a map of Texas. He found a small one and spread it on his desk. San Reale. It took him several minutes of searching, but he found the small town's location, to the north and west of San Antonio.

Office clerk Oliver Enright made arrangements for him and Harley to travel to San Antonio by train. From there, they would go by horseback to San Reale; a three-day ride, by Clint's estimation. They would take their horses with them in the stock car.

Clint had become acquainted with Harley when he joined the US cavalry at age seventeen. It was post–Civil War Texas when jobs were scarce, so he lied about his age and enlisted. For some unknown reason, Fry, who was the civilian scout, had taken an immediate liking to him. The scout had taken it upon himself to teach the green recruit all about surviving in a hard land. During their time together, Clint had learned all about Fry's adventurous spirit, too. The scout could claim a background as varied as one could find, including spending a few winters in the Rockies at the end of the beaver-trapping boom, followed by an excursion into Mexico in 1846 with General Taylor, then fighting at Pea Ridge with Colonel Dodge in 1862.

Clint found Harley at the Underwood stable sitting on an upside-down wooden bucket with a Winchester '76 in his hands. He was running a cloth swab through the barrel with a wire. Another Winchester lay to his left on a hay bale.

"Getting ready for another war?" Clint asked.

"I figure Lucas has something in mind. Pays to be ready."

Clint told Harley about the telegram and Ed Wilhoit's plea for help.

"Not like Ed Wilhoit to ask fer help," Harley said.

"That's my opinion, too. But I'm going to San Reale to check it out. Want to go along?"

"Guess so."

"That's good, because the arrangements have already been made."

With that settled, Clint's thoughts returned to the telegram's cryptic message. *You are involved.*

CHAPTER THREE

Clint lagged two horse lengths behind Harley as they rode toward San Reale. The old geezer wore his usual buckskin shirt, gray pants, and soft-brimmed leather hat. A pouch of strong tobacco was always nearby. Clint had decided on a faded red cotton shirt, black denims, and his old traveling hat, once white but now gray.

His Colt was holstered and strapped around his waist.

"How much did you pay for that packhorse?" Clint asked.

Harley was leading a packhorse he had bought from the San Antonio livery stable owner after dickering over the price for half the night.

"Got him fer thirty-one dollars. Made him throw in the pack gear in the deal."

Clint laughed. He knew that Harley had offered twenty-six dollars at the outset, but the owner had wanted thirty-seven dollars. Clint understood that it was a game both of the old-timers relished, while downing half a quart of Kentucky bourbon in the process.

"Hope he can make the trip," Clint said. "He looks pretty broke down to me."

"He'll do. I never got took on a horse deal in my life."

They had spent the first night in San Antonio where Clint had mapped out his plans and bought trail supplies: coffee, coffeepot, dried fruit, bacon and beans, a cooking pan and eating utensils. He splurged by spending seven of Underwood's dollars for a night at the Mission Hotel, while Harley, as was his custom, bedded down with the stock.

Come daybreak, they were in their saddles, and on the hard-packed stage road. The barren land through which they traveled was flat and arid. They were surrounded by a scattering of mesquite, scrub brush, and prickly-pear cactus. In the distance were low hills dotted with patches of green from which he felt a soft breeze blowing in to make the morning travel more tolerable. The hills soon became larger and the green patches of trees became more prevalent.

"This is the first time I've been in Texas since I left the Rangers," Clint said. "Lucas has had me in Colorado and Kansas most of the time. It's good to get back to familiar territory."

"Ain't changed all that much. Still hot and dry. Did your pa thank that drummer back in Kentucky for tellin' him about all the available land in Texas?"

Clint laughed. "I don't recall. I was only ten years old at the time. But I can tell you this. Getting out of those Kentucky hills and traveling a thousand miles in a mule-pulled wagon was an adventure I'll long remember. I wouldn't want to do it again. It liked to have killed my ma. But I guess that Cherokee blood back in her history must've taken care of her."

"Cherokee blood, eh?" Harley said. "That might account fer some of your peculiar ways of lookin' at things."

"I don't know how far back it went. Ma never talked much about it."

That time in his life seemed like centuries ago when he thought about it. In particular, the time he decided to pack a bag and leave home. That almost killed his ma, too, but she'd seen it coming and didn't object—at least to his face. Pa just stuffed a couple of dollars in his shirt pocket, patted him on the shoulder, and returned to his work.

Clint was fifteen years old at the time, approaching his top-out height of six feet three inches, strong and determined—but green as a garden snake. He'd been too young to fight in the War of Rebellion, so he worked at odd jobs wherever he could find them. After Lee's surrender at Appomattox, when jobs were scarce, he joined the Union cavalry to chase Comanche raiding parties and border bandits.

Then came the years of riding with the Texas Rangers. During that time, he was introduced to Lucas Underwood by an Austin businessman who said Lucas was on the lookout for tough, smart men for his detective agency. Clint hadn't been too anxious to leave the Rangers; he'd made too many friends among that bunch of fighting men to just up and ride away. Still, he listened to Underwood's persuasive spiel and the possibilities had an appeal. He left the Rangers with some regret and became a detective. Although he had always referred to himself as a troubleshooter.

CHAPTER FOUR

They were on their third day on the stage road between San Antonio and San Reale. The sun was high, with a few billowing clouds passing overhead. Clint felt at ease traveling through country that was becoming more and more isolated. He saw no one and passed few ranch houses. The ones he saw were set off in the distance several miles apart. This was wide-open country in which they were traveling. He saw a smattering of grass here and there mixed in among the wild growth, but it was scarce.

"There's no shortage of room around here for horses and longhorns, or anything else that took a notion to settle here," Clint said.

"Yep," Harley said. "That includes rattlers, wolves, coyotes, Kioways, and Comanches."

When they rode deeper into the Texas hill country, Clint began to recognize a few landmarks he hadn't seen in several years. "Some of these buttes and hills around here have a familiar look about them."

"Ought to. We patrolled this part of the country during the troubles in sixty-eight and sixty-nine."

"I remember us chasing after Wolf Eye. I wonder whatever happened to that old catamount."

"I would love to get him in my sights just one time."

"If memory serves, you did have him in your sights once, but missed."

"Bad powder," Harley said, stuffing a hunk of tobacco into

his cheek. "Hadn't been fer that bad powder, I'da nailed him fer sure."

"How far are we from that canyon where we found that bloody Comanche massacre?"

"Not far. Two days' ride, maybe three, west of here. Did you ever read any of them books that were writ about that massacree? I never knowed that place to have a name, but them book writers call the place Massacre Canyon."

"I've read a couple of them. Lieutenant McKendrick was behind that name. He told every newspaperman in the country about what he'd found in that canyon. And he wasn't beyond exaggerating some either. The book writers took his story and blew it up even more."

"You think there's anything to all that gold talk? Some folks say them Mexican bandits had *mucho* gold with them. Them book writers seemed to think so, too."

Clint shook his head and growled at his partner. "Hell, Harley, you were there. Did you see any gold? And if there was, somebody would've found it by now, don't you think?"

The little blue-eyed girl came to mind, too. The ranch where the cavalry had left her should be nearby. "That little girl we found at the canyon that day, she would be what, around nineteen, twenty years old by now?"

"About that, I reckon. You ain't never going to forget about that little young'un, are you? You talk about her all the time."

"I think about her a lot. She sure had a terrible start in life. Her folks were killed, and she was kidnapped by the killers. I figure they were going to sell her to some rich *senor* down in Mexico. Then to top it off, she was witness to a bloody Indian attack. It can't get much worse than that for a youngster."

Clint shook his head in amazement. "I never understood how she got out of all that alive."

He was about to ask Harley a question, when he saw the old

scout bring his horse to a sudden halt.

"Tobacco smoke," Harley said. "We best be cautious."

Clint then saw the flickering of Buck's ears, and felt the horse's muscles tense beneath him. His instincts took over as he ducked low and veered off the road. A shot rang out from a stand of trees to his left. A bullet hit the pommel of his saddle, almost knocking him off the horse. More shots were fired.

Harley was already moving, riding low. Clint steadied himself in the saddle and followed the scout's lead. They spurred their mounts in different directions: Clint went hard left, Harley hard right. Then both turned and charged straight at the stand of trees, still ducking low. Clint had been in situations like this before with Harley and acted on pure instinct. Both began shooting at the spot where the powder smoke lingered.

Clint spotted two men running for their horses. One of them, a heavy, broad-shouldered man carrying a rifle, stopped in mid stride to take one more shot. He turned, put a Winchester to his shoulder, and took aim. That impulsive decision would be his worst—and his last. Clint pointed his Colt at the man and squeezed the trigger. The bullet went through the bushwhacker's shirt pocket. A spray of blood exploded outward as the ambusher collapsed on his face, his arms outstretched. The man had dropped ten feet from his horse and a clean getaway.

Clint could hear the sound of a running horse in the distance as the other bushwhacker made good his escape. The second ambusher rode away and left his partner dying in the hot Texas dust. Clint hurried over to the downed shooter, put a foot under his body, and flipped him over on his back. The man's eyes were glazed over and his breathing was shallow.

"I'm . . . hit bad . . . ain't I?"

Clint gave him a straight answer. "You're hit bad all right. Why did you ambush us?"

The man's body shuddered as he struggled to speak. "Fifty

. . . dollars . . . to . . . kill . . . both . . ." A gurgling sound came from deep in the man's throat, then he died.

Harley rode up to his side. "Know him?"

"Can't say that I do." Clint riffled through the man's pockets, found a few coins, a sack of tobacco, and two twenty-dollar gold pieces.

Harley rounded up the dead man's horse and threw his body across the saddle. He lashed him on with rawhide strips, then slapped the horse on the rump, and sent it scampering away down the trail.

"Don't reckon we have time to deal with him." He cut off a hunk of tobacco with a long knife and stuck it in his jaw. He pointed the knife toward the clump of trees that had concealed the shooters. "From the looks of things, them two bushwhackers had been hunkered down behind them trees fer a long while."

"They were waiting for us," Clint said. He then related what the man told him with his dying breath. He tossed one of the twenty-dollar gold pieces to Harley. "Somebody thinks we're worth a hundred dollars dead."

Harley stuck the coin in his mouth and bit down on it. "And you always called me a worthless old coot."

CHAPTER FIVE

Clint and Harley rode into the town of San Reale near dusk on the third day. It was a small town with a population of around six or seven hundred people that had sprung up by necessity, being the central trading center in the midst of widespread cattle country.

"Does this town look familiar to you?" Clint asked, as they rode down Main Street past an eclectic mixture of adobe, wood-framed, and stone buildings. He spotted a barbershop, harness shop, bank, and several other small businesses one would expect to find in cattle country.

"Yep," Harley said. "I've seed about a hundred that look just like it. Some bigger, some not so big."

Clint counted eight side streets angling off in both directions from the main street. A dozen or more saddled horses stood at hitching rails along the street, stamping at the hard-packed earth while they waited for their owners to return. They rode past the Sundown Saloon where half a dozen scruffy-looking men were loitering on the front steps with smokes hanging out of their mouths.

"I do believe those gents are givin' us the evil eye," Harley said.

"Strangers are always cause for speculation, I guess." Clint nodded in their direction and kept moving. He didn't look back, but he could sense their stares boring a hole in him.

A little farther along, Clint spotted a man sitting on a bench in front of the Sutton Brothers' Mercantile store. The man was whittling on a piece of scrap wood. Clint pulled Buck to a stop in front of the whittler. He took off his sweat-ringed hat, and ran a hand through his hair.

"Say partner, can you point us toward the sheriff's office?"

The man had a sizable pile of wood shavings at his feet. Clint figured he'd been sitting there most of the afternoon.

The whittler lowered his piece of wood and pointed to his left. "Down the street on the right, next to the feed store."

Clint nodded his thanks. "We'll need a room, too. Is there a hotel in town?"

"There's Martha Ann's Boardinghouse down the way a piece. I reckon she could fix you up. It's the big white two-story building past the sheriff's office. She puts on a good table, too."

That sounded good, but first things first. Clint needed to look up Ed Wilhoit and let him know he and Harley were in town. And to find out what his urgent message was all about.

"You go on ahead and find Ed," Harley said. "I'll find us a stable and look after our bags and the horses. I'll join up with you later."

The reddish glow beyond the darkening hills lifted Clint's spirits. He was beginning to feel a little renewed as he walked through the small town. He passed a grain store, Lulu's Café, and Rainey's Boot Repair shop. Farther down the street, he walked past a shotgun-style building with the shingle of Doctor Hosea Wiggins hanging on the door.

Ahead on the opposite side of the street he spotted the feed store and crossed over. Like the man said, the sheriff's office was next door. He stepped into the office where a burly man with a three-day growth was seated behind a cluttered desk trimming his fingernails with a small folding knife. The man jumped as the door opened.

"I'm here to see Sheriff Wilhoit," Clint announced. "Is he around?"

"Who're you?" the man asked in a disagreeable tone. "And why do you want to see the sheriff?"

"I have some business to discuss with him. Is he close by?"

The office was dimly lit with a single coal-oil lantern hanging from the ceiling. A wood-burning stove sat in the back corner with a coffeepot perched on top. One side wall was covered with an array of yellowed, out-of-date wanted posters. On the other side wall was a six-foot-tall wooden gun case that held two rifles and two double-barreled shotguns. A chain ran through the trigger guards of the weapons and was locked to a hasp on the side of the cabinet. In short, to Clint, it looked like every other small-town sheriff's office he'd seen.

"Mister, my name is Deputy Sam Elder. I said I'd like to know your name, and what business you might have with the sheriff."

Clint saw the badge on the man's vest, so he decided to give the man a benefit of the doubt. After all, he realized he'd walked in unannounced, looking like a grungy drifter. But he also decided not to give away too much information up front.

"My name is Ramsay. I was in the area and I thought I'd stop in and speak to the sheriff about a couple of things. Any objections?"

Elder leaned back in the chair and said, "Nope, I ain't got no objections a-tall. But I'm real sorry to have to tell you that we buried the sheriff this afternoon. A no-good puncher kilt him yesterday as he was riding outside of town."

CHAPTER SIX

Ed Wilhoit dead.

While they hadn't been what he would call close friends, the news still hit Clint hard. Ed had needed his help, and he'd come too late. Then the other sobering thought surfaced again. *You are involved.*

Clint hadn't been offered a chair, so he still stood in front of the desk digesting what he'd heard. "It sounds like you might know who killed the sheriff. Who was it? How did it happen?"

"I don't know that it's any of your concern who kilt him, stranger." Elder straightened up in his chair and pointed a finger at him. "We can take care of our own business around here without any butting in by drifters. You best be moving along while you can."

Clint took a step around the desk toward the deputy and looked down at him. "Do you want to answer my question in a civil manner, or do you want me to ask it again?"

Elder looked away and began fiddling with his folding knife. "Uh, well, I got the killer locked up back there in a cell. We cotched him right after he shot Wilhoit."

"Why?"

"Why what?"

"Why did this man kill the sheriff?"

Elder shook his head. "Don't know the particulars. He was always hanging around the sheriff whenever he came to town. Maybe they quarreled, I don't know. I expect the judge and jury will figure that out, if he lasts that long. There's a lot of sentiment out there for a necktie party."

"I want to see your prisoner."

"You ain't got no business seeing the prisoner. You best ride on out of here like I said."

Clint unbuckled his gun belt and laid it on the desk. "I want to talk to him for a few minutes. I won't be long." He then walked through the rear door to the cell area.

"Hey, you can't do that. The judge said . . ."

But Clint was already through the door. There were two cells facing each other with an eight-foot walkway between them. A man was stretched out on a bunk attached to the adobe wall. The inmate stirred and turned toward the door when Clint entered the cell area. He swung his feet over to the floor and jumped up.

"Ramsay," he hollered. "Is that you?"

Clint walked closer to the cell to get a closer look at the prisoner who had called him by name. He broke out into a big grin when he recognized him.

"Waco," he said with a smile on his face. Clint couldn't believe the man accused of killing Ed was Waco Wallace, a man who had ridden with him as a Texas Ranger not too long ago. He had changed very little during that time. He was still the shaggy-haired, bowlegged, forty-year-old man who looked like a choirboy.

"You shot Ed?" Clint asked.

"Oh, hell no, I never shot Ed. That bumpkin in there wearing the deputy's badge is one of Jake Polk's lackeys, and he locked me up because I was handy."

"Tell me what happened."

Waco grabbed the steel bars with both hands and squeezed his face between them as he talked. "I own a little spread two hours east of town. Not a big place, but it has promise. Ellie and me—I'm married now—have worked hard to make something out of it. Every week or so I come to town to pick up supplies and to visit with Ed and have a drink or two. Yesterday when it came time to leave, Ed rode out with me. I was in a wagon with the supplies, and Ed was on his horse. When we came to the fork at Willow Creek, I turned off east toward my place, while Ed took the other direction. We said our good-byes and moved on. I had rode a ways when I heard a rifle shot. Then I heard another one. That concerned me since it came from the general direction of where Ed was headed. So I turned the wagon around and went to check on it. That's when I found Ed on the ground dead. One bullet had hit him in the upper chest, and another one had hit him in his shoulder."

"You didn't see anyone?"

"Not a living soul. And never heard nothing else either. I beat it back to town and found Elder—that's the deputy in yonder—and told him what happened. Me and Elder and two other men went out there, and the next thing I know he arrested me and locked me up."

"Why did he arrest you? What evidence did he have?"

"Damned if I know. He just looked around and said, 'You're under arrest.' "

"You're sure the deputy isn't hiding something from you? Some piece of evidence that points to you?"

"I can't say for certain, but how could he? He just pulled a gun right there on the spot and hauled me back here. I've got to get outta here, Clint. Ellie will be worried sick."

"I'll try. No promises."

Clint left the cell area and went back into the office and saw that the deputy had company. A bear of a man was standing in front of the desk. He was above medium height, maybe six feet tall, muscular, and had a wide face with protruding brows that were covered with thick black hair. He wore a blue suit over a buttoned vest. He might have been forty-five years old, if that. Like the deputy, a scowl covered his face.

"That's the man, Mister Polk."

Clint picked up his gun belt and strapped it on. He looked over at the man. "Who're you?"

"I'm Jake Polk. I'm a city council member in this town, and I could have you arrested for what you just did."

"Maybe, but you won't. In fact, if you don't let Wallace out of that cell in the next fifteen minutes, you're going to have the biggest problem this town has ever seen. I think we would first sue this bumbling deputy here, then the mayor, then the city council. There might even be one or two more we'd add for good measure."

"Wha . . . what do you mean, sue us? Just who the hell are you to talk to me that way?"

"My name is Clint Ramsay. I work for the Underwood Detective Agency. I've just spoken with Waco Wallace, and I know the whole story. How this so-called deputy put a man behind bars on trumped-up charges. I know a railroading when I see one. I plan to contact Lucas Underwood and have his lawyers start drawing up the papers."

Polk mumbled something that Clint couldn't understand.

"Your deputy here arrested an innocent man because he's too lazy to search for evidence of the real killer." Clint hesitated for a few seconds, then added, "Or did he have orders not to look any further?"

Clint noticed the deputy give Polk a quick glance at his comment. He continued: "Whatever the reason, your deputy forced Waco to remain in jail while he sat here trimming his fingernails. The lawyers will have a field day with this one. Better get your cash box out, Councilman."

Polk glared at Clint, then turned to the deputy. "Go unlock the cell and turn him loose." He then looked back at Clint.

"What's an Underwood man doing in San Reale, if you don't mind me asking? You couldn't have come here because of that two-by-four rancher."

"Don't mind saying at all. Ed Wilhoit sent for me. He said he needed my help."

"Ed said he needed help? I can't imagine why. We have a peaceful little town here."

"I have a different impression of your peaceful little town. Your sheriff has been killed by a bushwhacker, and my partner and I were shot at earlier today on our ride into town. I had to kill one of them in the scrape. The other one hightailed it when we started shooting back. And now I find you've jailed an innocent man without even bothering to search for the real culprit."

"Just taking precautions," Polk said, while rolling a smoke. "That's why I came over here. To have Wallace released."

At about that time Elder brought Waco out of the jail area. Elder opened a desk drawer and retrieved his prisoner's gun belt. He handed it over to Waco without looking him in the eye.

"Where's my wagon, you miserable coyote? And there better not be anything missing. If there is, I'm taking it outta your scaly hide."

"Take it easy, Waco," Clint said. "I've already told these gentlemen the Underwood lawyers will be looking into this on your behalf. Some judges don't appreciate jailing a man without a reason. While they're at it, the lawyers might find a few more interesting things about this peaceful little town. In fact, I might find a few more interesting things about this peaceful little town before I leave."

Clint saw Polk's jaws tighten and his fists clinch, but he didn't respond to the veiled threats. Instead, he turned and marched out the door without looking back.

Clint took Waco by the arm and followed Polk out the door.

They stood on the boardwalk and watched the councilman disappear into the dark.

"You know something funny, Waco? Neither the deputy, nor Polk, bothered to ask about the bushwhacker I told them I shot. You'd think they'd be a little curious."

"Maybe they already knew about it," Waco said.

"That was my thought, too."

Then they saw Harley walking toward them.

"Well, bless my soul, who do we have here?" Harley said, grabbing Waco in a bear hug. "Whur'd you round up this shorthorn?"

Clint gave him an abbreviated version of the events that took place in the sheriff's office.

"Ed was killed, huh?"

Waco nodded. "Ambushed."

Clint pointed toward Lulu's Café. "Let's go get a meal and talk this over."

CHAPTER SEVEN

The three men entered the long, narrow café where several coal-oil lanterns were throwing an eerie luster on the café's dull adobe walls. Clint spotted an empty table near the rear of the café. Lulu seemed to have a thriving business as most of the tables in the place were occupied. A few of the patrons glanced their way. Waco in particular received more than his share of dirty looks. A tall busty woman with big black eyes and a dark complexion spotted them at the table and came over. She stood with her hands clasped behind her back.

"You look like beefsteak men," she said. "We have three big ones back there with your names carved in them."

"Then you'd better get them out here in a hurry before somebody else with our names show up," Clint said. "And bring along a pot of hot coffee."

"Somebody kills Ed, and then somebody tries to kill you. A coincidence you think?" Waco asked.

Harley shook his head. "Tracks don't read that way fer me."

"The folks around here thought Ed was a good sheriff. He had to bust a few heads every now and then, but that's about it. He didn't go out of his way to roust people. He let the Saturday-night cowboys have their fun within reason."

The dark-haired woman returned and laid the platters in front of them. "I threw on some fried potatoes for good measure." She set a pot of coffee at Clint's elbow, leaned over his shoulder and whispered, "My name is Lulu in case you're wondering." She then sashayed away, glancing back at him over her shoulder.

Clint grinned as he watched her leave the table, then turned his attention back to Waco.

"Did Ed ever tell you anything that might explain why he sent for me?" Clint asked. "More to the point, the telegram said it was something that I was involved in. Do you have any idea what it could be?"

"Ed was not much of a one to talk, but around three or four weeks ago, he said there was a man who came to him with an idea that was going to make them both rich. He didn't say who it was, or what it was all about, but he was excited about it."

"Did he ever mention it again?"

"Just once. That was on the day he was killed. Ed said the deal wasn't turning out to be what he thought it was. He seemed kinda worried about the whole thing."

"Turns out he orta been worried," Harley said.

Waco looked around the café, lowered his voice, and said, "That Jake Polk you saw over at the jail. You had better watch out for him, Clint. It won't set easy with him, you backing him down like that."

"What's his business in town?"

"He runs the freight outfit. He has several toughs working for him, and I'm not talking about his teamsters. There were a couple other small freight lines that tried to make a go of it in town, but all of them ran into trouble along the way and pulled out."

"Man-made trouble?" Harley asked.

"I'd say so. Trouble that Polk never had."

"I'll keep an eye out. Who was Ed close to? Who were his friends in town?"

"He didn't have a lot of friends. He kept to hisself most of the time. Him and Marva over at the Sundown Saloon saw a lot of each other. Maybe one or two others."

Clint concluded that the sheriff had kept close to his vest whatever information he had. And, after meeting his deputy, he thought Ed's caution was a sound decision. The saloon woman in particular might be worth a visit.

"What're you going to do from here?" Waco asked. "You going to hang around for a while, or move on?"

"The fact somebody tried to kill us today means something," Clint said. "They might go for another try at us, or they might feel safe knowing that Ed is out of the way and can't talk to us. We'll hang around for a few days and see what develops."

Waco stood and held out his hand. "I'm glad you two showed up when you did. If I can help you, I'm at the Bar W out east of here. I've got two pretty salty hands on the place and we'll come a running if you need us."

Clint and Harley stood and shook Waco's hand and bade him good-bye. Clint then dropped some coins on the table, and they left the café together. He knew that Ed's telegram asking for help, and then finding that he had been killed, meant one thing. Trouble.

CHAPTER EIGHT

Clint walked down Main Street to Martha Ann's Boarding-house. He began to feel the tight muscles along his shoulders and neck beginning to loosen somewhat. His left shoulder seemed to have recovered to full movement. Harley had gone to bed down with the horses at the livery stable. A banjo played a rousing tune in the distance, and a small dog barked in answer, not quite keeping in time with the banjo player. A few children ran around in the dark, playing hide-and-seek, laughing, and yelling.

He had to keep reminding himself that while the small-town sounds were comforting, somewhere close by was a killer, or killers, who liked to shoot from behind trees and rocks.

He entered the front room and took a moment to acquaint himself with the place. The room had several upholstered chairs that faced a large stone fireplace. Off to the side sat a hand-hewn table holding a pen and writing materials. Several colorful western-themed paintings were scattered along the four walls. A painter's wooden easel with a blank canvas attached sat next to the fireplace. It appeared an artist had taken up temporary lodging on the premises.

A short, stout woman, wearing an oversized white apron, stood behind the registration desk. She had crinkles around her brown eyes and a pleasant look on her face. She appeared to be in her mid-fifties.

"Ma'am, I need a room for a few nights. And a bath, too, if

it's not too late."

He wouldn't have blamed her if she had shooed him out to the street knowing how shabby he must look. But she didn't.

"We can take care of all that for you," she said. "That'll be three dollars for the room and six bits for the bath in advance. It'll take Juan about twenty minutes to prepare the bath, so you'll have time to stow your gear in your room. Your room will be number two oh four on the second floor facing the street. The bath house is at the rear of the building through that door."

Clint retrieved the money from his shirt pocket and dropped it on the desk, then signed the guest register. "Thanks, ma'am. I'll be back in about twenty minutes."

Later, Clint sat in the wooden tub with hot soapy water bubbling up to his chin. "Another bucket of hot water, Juan. And see if you can round up another sliver of that soap." He was content to sit in the warm water and let the miles of dusty riding wash off his tired, aching body. He even asked Juan to trim his hair as he relaxed in the tub.

While Juan was working on his hair, he said, "I'm a stranger in town. What would I find outside of San Reale?"

"Ranches, rattlesnakes, mesquite scrub," Juan replied in passable English. "*Mucho* cattle."

"What ranches are around here?"

"Two big ranches north. The Holliday Ranch and O'Harrow's Big O." He waved a hand around. "Smaller ranches everywhere."

"Anything else?"

"Not much, *senor.* Saint Anthony's Mission maybe."

Clint remained in the tub until the hot water cooled, then he got out, dried off, and dressed in a clean outfit. He left his dirty, stinking traveling clothes with Juan to launder. Back in his room, he bounced on the soft mattress, trying it out, looking forward to a restful night's sleep. Tomorrow he knew he would have to go find out why Ed Wilhoit sent for him—and why it got him killed.

CHAPTER NINE

Clint slept late the following morning. He took his time as he put on a clean blue shirt with a white trim around the collar, and a pair of spotless black denims. Juan had cleaned the grime from his black boots and had put a brush to his traveling hat. The sun was way up, and he had no idea of the time. The feather mattress bed had swallowed him up whole. Even though he had awakened feeling refreshed, he wasn't at ease, knowing what might lie ahead.

The same woman was behind the desk as was there the previous night. She was bent over the registration desk writing on a pad when he came down the stairs. She looked up at the sound of his boots on the wooden floor. He smiled when he saw her double take as he walked toward her.

"Sakes alive," she said. "You don't even resemble the man who came in here last night."

He smiled and said, "Anything left in the dining room, or am I too late?"

"I've saved some flapjacks and a half dozen eggs for you in the kitchen, so get on back there and tell Louise I said to fix you up."

As he headed for the kitchen, he noticed a man near the fireplace sitting at the painter's easel. The man appeared to be studying the blank canvas as if a beautiful scene would appear if he stared at it long enough. The man was around forty years of age or so, standing five feet eight or nine, and weighing perhaps

44

one hundred and fifty pounds. He puffed on a long-stemmed pipe and played with his bow tie as he stared at the canvas.

He noticed Clint looking in his direction.

"Sir," the painter said, "my name is Robert Shorter. Would you like to have your portrait painted? It will be most inexpensive, and I can have it finished in an hour. We can use our imagination. We can put you on a horse, or have you fighting off Indians, or put you atop the Alamo with Bowie and Crockett."

Clint laughed. "You're trying to make a diamond out of coal dust, my friend. Maybe another time."

Shorter bowed his head and said, "Yes, sir, maybe another time."

He worked through the huge breakfast Louise brought him, then hoofed it down to the livery stable where he found Harley fiddling with the bundles he had taken from the packhorse.

"You still babying that nag?" Clint asked.

"Got us this far. I 'spect he'll get us back when the time comes."

"If he lives that long."

Harley cut off a hunk of tobacco and stuffed it in his jaw. "Don't go belittling my purchase."

Clint shook his head, then said, "Why don't you nose around town and see what gossip you can pick up. I'm going to look up Ed's lady friend over at the saloon. Maybe he told her something that might shed some light on his death."

"I've got this funny feeling that not everything is as it seems in this town. You best be careful and watch your backside."

Clint turned to walk away when a rider on a mustang raced by him, creating a thick swirl of dust as he passed. Clint jumped back and watched as the rider stopped in front of Doctor Wiggins's office, leaped off the horse, and ran inside. A few minutes later, the rider and a stooped man carrying a black medical bag hurried out of the office. The older man climbed into a one-seat, canvas-topped buggy. He popped his whip at the horse and followed the rider out of town. Both were pushing their horses hard.

"I wonder what that's all about," Clint said. "Let's wander over that way and see what we can find out."

They walked over to where three men stood talking in low voices. "Did someone get thrown from a horse, or something?" Clint asked.

One of the men took a cigarette from his mouth and said in a slow drawl, "Best we can figure, somebody plugged Justus Holliday while he was out tending to his herd. Lang Potter, that's the puncher who came for the doc, said the old man was hit in the leg. He weren't sure how serious he is."

"Holliday?" Clint asked.

"Holliday owns a big spread north of town. Once worked for him."

"There seems to be a lot of shooting around this here little town," Harley said.

The man looked at him and walked away without speaking.

CHAPTER TEN

Clint had learned that Ed's friend, Marva, lived in room 2A above the Sundown Saloon. He found a back entrance to the saloon and walked up the stairs. He scanned the narrow hallway looking for room numbers. There were three rooms on each side. Room 2A was located on the right side of the hallway. He eased up to the door so he could hear any movement inside the room.

Hearing nothing, he tapped twice on the door. Then again.

From inside, a woman shouted, "Go away, whoever you are."

He tapped again, and said in a high-pitched voice, "Message for you, Miss Marva."

That did the trick. He heard footsteps approaching and a key turning in a lock. The door opened and a tall woman with long red hair stood in the doorway. She appeared to be in her mid-to-late thirties, wearing a floor-length red robe. When she saw him, a stranger, she tried to slam the door in his face, but Clint was prepared for the maneuver, and had a boot between the door and the jamb.

He reached into his shirt pocket and took out a ten-dollar greenback. He held it out like a carrot on a stick. "Marva, I need to talk with you for a few minutes. Nothing but talk. Can I come in?"

She looked him up and down through the crack in the door, then grabbed the money, and stepped aside. "Who are you? What do you want?"

"My name is Ramsay. I came to San Reale to see Ed Wilhoit and found out he'd been killed. I also learned that he was a friend of yours. I thought you might be able to help me find his killer."

"I've heard rumors that a man was in town asking questions about Ed. Ten dollars will get you an hour, so time's a wasting. If talk's all you want, have at it."

The small room had the barest of necessities: bed, dresser, washstand, and a tall wooden armoire with its two hinged doors standing open. A quick glance into it revealed that Marva favored the color red. She walked over to the bed, sat down and crossed her legs, letting the top of the robe fall open, revealing not only a glance at her obvious assets, but a beautiful oval turquoise piece hanging on a silver chain.

"Do you have any thoughts on who killed Ed, or why? Everyone calls this a peaceful town, so when a sheriff is killed, it should create a few rumors and speculations about who might've pulled the trigger. Have you heard anything?"

She stood and walked over to the washstand and took a whiskey bottle off a lower shelf. "Want a drink? Or is it too early for you?" She poured a water glass to the brim then drank half of it in one swallow. She turned back to him. "All I know is he started acting different a few weeks ago. At first he was . . . I don't know . . . excited, I guess you'd call it. He was that way up until a few days ago, when he changed. The excitement was gone. In its place was . . ." Her voice trailed off.

"Fear?" Clint asked.

"No . . . not so much fear as disappointment. Or maybe he was discouraged about something. Anyway, it was something like that. He was different, that's all I know."

"Did he ever mention any names?"

"He never mentioned a name to me. But Ed didn't talk a lot. I just noticed that he started acting different, so that told me that he was worried. He began riding out of town more often, too, always carrying a double-barreled shotgun with him wherever he went. He never used to do that. Whatever it was bothering him, he took it serious."

"Is there anything else the sheriff might've done, or said, that would help me? Anything at all?"

"He once said that he had got hisself all mixed up in something that he should have left alone. I don't have any idea what it was, but something about it went bad, and that's when he changed. The last time I saw him he said he needed help. He said he'd sent a telegram to somebody he knew way back when. I imagine that's why you're here."

"When was the last time you saw Ed?"

She turned her back to him and thought for a moment. "The night before he was killed. He came by for a few minutes and we talked, then he left."

"Where did he hang his hat when he wasn't with you?"

"He had a room at the back of the sheriff's office. Wasn't much, but it suited him just fine. I never heard him complain about it."

Clint walked over to her and took hold of her arm. "I'm going to find Ed's killer, you can count on it. One more question, then I'll leave. Are you keeping anything from me?" He watched for a reaction and saw a distinct flicker of her eyelids. He felt the muscles of her arm tighten.

She jerked her arm from his grip and walked away. She reached for the whiskey glass and poured another glass full. Clint grabbed her by the wrist again and swung her around to face him, spilling half of the whiskey onto the floor. "You're holding something back, aren't you, Marva? Tell me what you know about Ed's death."

"Nothing," she hissed. "I don't know a thing about it."

He decided to try a new tack. He released her wrist and took a step back. "Just so you know. The Underwood Detective Agency has put a one-thousand-dollar reward out on his killer. It can be yours if you help us catch him. Think about it. I'll be over at Martha Ann's Boardinghouse if your memory improves."

Clint was confident by her reactions that Marva knew more than she was telling. He had no way of knowing what that something was, but he was convinced she was hiding something from him. Maybe the seed he'd planted about a reward would produce fruit down the line.

A more sobering thought also occurred to him; he had no idea where he'd come up with a thousand dollars if it came to that.

CHAPTER ELEVEN

Calico Holliday paced back and forth in her father's bedroom with an anxious look on her face. Her father, Justus Holliday, lay in the bed with his head propped up on two fluffy goose-down pillows. She was still struggling with the vision of him lying in bed. She couldn't recall ever seeing him when he was not a vigorous, robust figure of a man, shouting out orders, or out on the range doing the work of two cowhands. Seeing him forced to lie still was difficult for her to handle. She was filled with anger at the very thought of someone shooting him while he'd been working his cattle on his own range.

"I'll be fine," Justus told her over and over. "Doctor Wiggins said the bullet missed everything that was important. But I can't stay in this bed any longer or I'll go madder than a cow chowing down on loco weed. So tell August to hurry up with those crutches."

"You just be more careful the next time you go confronting strangers," she said.

"I guess you're right, honey. But all I was doing was bunching a few strays along Line Creek. The stranger I spotted was on the far side of the creek, and looking back on it, I'm surprised I even saw him. It appeared as if he was making an effort to hide. I just stopped what I was doing and watched him for a few minutes, then decided it might be prudent to see what he was up to. The next thing I knew I was flat on the ground with a bullet in my leg."

Her father had come to Texas from an aristocratic, genteel home in Philadelphia, Pennsylvania. According to her mother, he had always been the adventurer of the family and had caused the rest of the Hollidays more than their share of consternation. If not being chastised for his untoward behavior with his rowdy friends, he'd often been rebuked for his long unexplained absences from home. After all, Justus had been born into a Pennsylvania lineage that boasted of maternal roots going all the way back to the Mayflower. Certain deportment had been expected of him. Their mother had been a Pennsylvania Abbott. Nothing more needed to be said.

One evening as the Hollidays sat around the crackling fireplace discussing the day's activities, Justus, nineteen years old at the time, just up and announced, "I'm going west tomorrow." And he did. That was thirty-eight years ago. Following the end of war with Mexico in 1848, Justus had the good fortune to meet Sarah McIntire, who tied an anchor to his roving tail, and brought a measure of stability to his life.

"Do you think he was a rustler scouting our herd?" Calico asked.

"I can't say. Joe Peterson says there are no cattle or horses missing as far as he can tell. The men on the range have been on the lookout and haven't seen anyone since then. Just as a precaution though, I want you to stay close by for a few days. I don't want you to be riding too far from the ranch house until we're sure you'll be safe."

"I won't be kept a prisoner in my own home." Then Calico added in an angry voice, "I've got a rifle and I know how to use it. If I see any strangers snooping around here, I'll make them sorry."

Justus grinned. "Just do as I say. Stay close by for a while."

"But it's getting worse around here, Dad. First the sheriff is killed, and now you've been shot in your own backyard."

"It's heartening to see you take it so hard." He reached out a hand to her and continued, "Maybe it's your generation that will see an end to these callous deeds. In the meantime, it's a fact of life where we live, so you might as well get used to it."

"Get used to seeing my father get shot! I don't think so. If anyone comes snooping around here they'll wish they hadn't."

CHAPTER TWELVE

Clint sat on a bench in front of the feed store with a toothpick stuck in his mouth. He stretched out his legs on the boardwalk and watched the townsfolk go about their day-to-day affairs. Harley joined him after a while and took a seat in front of him on the edge of the boardwalk. Up and down the street, people rushed this way and that way: a wagon had pulled up to the mercantile for a load of supplies, and the stagecoach for San Antonio departed the depot leaving a choking dust cloud in its wake. Young children ran about in the street chasing each other, with a small dog barking and chasing after them. Deputy Sam Elder made himself conspicuous as he stood in front of the barbershop, staring in their direction.

"I think maybe the deputy took exception to my interfering in his business last night," Clint said.

"Don't blame him. You're bad about that."

"That Polk fellow bears watching, too. He was a little too slick for my tastes. And I think the saloon woman Ed had been seeing knows more than she's telling."

"You're a suspicious so-and-so, ain't you?"

"I learned it from you, you old codger." Clint took off his hat and shooed away a fly buzzing around his head. "I kinda stepped out on a limb with this Marva. I told her the man who killed Ed had a thousand-dollar reward on his head. Maybe she'll start thinking about that and want to talk."

"You got a thousand dollars?"

"Nope."

"Didn't think so."

Clint tossed the toothpick aside and said, "Let's go over to the sheriff's office while the deputy is out and do a little snooping around."

Harley stood and said, "You like being a detective, don't you? You're partial to snooping around, and sticking your nose in other folk's business."

"It's a living," Clint said. "Marva said Ed lived in a room at the rear of the office."

They walked through a rear door of the office into the room where Ed had set up his living quarters. The room was about ten feet square with just enough room for a cot, a washstand, and an old apple crate standing on its end that served as a place to keep a few odds and ends. A series of nails on the wall held two spare shirts and a spare pair of pants. A framed picture of a mounted cavalry unit sat on top of the apple crate. Clint picked it up and looked at it. He recognized it as a photograph of the unit in which he and Harley had served with Ed. He handed it to Harley.

Harley looked at it and shook his head. "The high point of his life, I 'spect."

Clint looked inside the apple crate where he found several tattered magazines and books. He picked up one of the dime novels and looked at it. The title of the book was *The Massacre Canyon Incident, or, How Wolf Eye Sprung His Trap*. The book had a colorful painted cover with Indians and Mexican men fighting hand to hand, wagons burning, and horses running amok in the background. He picked up a second book with a similar cover. This one was entitled *The Lost Massacre Canyon Gold*. Both were written by a man called Bison Bob.

He held up the books for Harley to see. "It appears Ed liked to read about the massacre."

Under the cot Clint found a ragged-edged copy of *The National Police Gazette*. The magazine advertised its cover story as "The Truth About the Gold of Massacre Canyon." He replaced the reading materials and continued his search. There was little in the room that helped. He found an old leather bag with "3rd Cavalry" burned on the flap. Inside were a few ribbons and an assortment of cloths, polish, and other items essential to a well-kept cavalryman. He looked in all the nooks and crannies, under the mattress, and inside the pillow.

Neither of them found anything they took to be important.

Outside on the boardwalk, Clint nodded his head toward the north end of town. "I plan to take a gander out north of here. There's a cattle ranch out that way called the Holliday Ranch that has popped up in my conversations a couple of times. I think it might be worth taking a ride out there to see if there's a connection between the rancher's shooting and Ed's. I'll see you back here later tonight, or tomorrow morning. You just keep nosing around while I'm gone. And keep an eye on a tall redheaded woman who might decide to wander away from the Sundown Saloon. I'd like to know where she goes if she decides to ramble around."

"I'll watch," Harley said. "I kinda like redheads."

"I know. That's why I suggested it."

CHAPTER THIRTEEN

Marva sat on the bed in her room thinking about the conversation she'd had with the Underwood detective—and thinking too about Jake Polk. She and Jake had begun meeting on the sly soon after his arrival in San Reale a little more than a year ago. Then three months ago he suggested they meet away from the Sundown; away from prying eyes. He didn't explain why, but neither did she question his reasons. She figured that after becoming a councilman, he didn't want his name besmirched by consorting with a woman of her particular profession. That was fine by her. As long as he kept the money flowing, she was open to anything he suggested. If she played her cards right, he just might be her ticket out of this one-horse town.

Still, she'd always been curious about Polk's past. Few people just showed up in a town like San Reale with a pocketful of money. Polk had been in town just one week when he bought out Nathan Anderson's freight line lock, stock, and barrel. He soon became a prominent and influential fixture in town. But she had her sources. After all, the men who worked for him were frequent visitors to her boudoir, too. One of them, Anse Hocker, had ridden into town with him on that first day and was rumored to be his number-two man. Hocker was a dirty, obscene, and mean man. But he liked to talk when he had a few too many drinks. Marva made certain she always had a full bottle around when Hocker knocked on her door.

One night after he had drained a bottle, he began talking. He didn't seem to be aware that she was in the room when he stared at the floor and began to ramble on about the past. She had listened with rapt attention.

"They're gonna catch up with us sure as shooting," he said. "And when they do, they'll hang us. Jesse and Frank have took on new names, and are on the run from the Pinkertons. Cole is in Stillwater prison after that Northfield bank job, and all the other old Quantrill men are on the run. They'll hang us sure if they catch up to us. I don't want to hang. I'll go out shooting, but I don't want no rope around my neck."

Over time, in his drunken state, Marva had heard Hocker mention a train holdup somewhere in Oklahoma, and a bank robbery at a place called Clay County. He once talked about something terrible that happened in Lawrence, Kansas, but she had no idea what he meant by it. She didn't know whether to press her luck by asking him questions when he got into one of those states, or pretend she never heard. She chose to pretend he'd never said a word and kept it all to herself.

But those statements stuck with her: changed names, Quantrill, Frank and Jesse, and train holdups. She learned enough from Hocker to suspect that one person he often mentioned was Jake Polk—and that Polk, like Hocker, was a wanted man. She had become convinced that the broad-shouldered, black-browed Polk was the kind of man who would kill a sheriff and never give it a second thought.

She walked over to the mirror and took a good look at her fading beauty. She touched her hair and saw the gray beginning to peek through the red. She noticed the wrinkles around her eyes and mouth.

I'm growing old with nothing to show for it.

She spun around and sat down on the bed, where she began to think about what she could do with one thousand dollars.

Chapter Fourteen

Clint rode north for an hour before he spotted the adobe mission Juan had mentioned. What was it? Saint Anthony's Mission? It had a five-foot-high wooden cross atop the structure to differentiate it from the other adobe buildings that surrounded it. There were a dozen or so huts of varying sizes scattered about along a wide dusty street. A few women sat in the shade of an ancient live-oak tree cutting vegetables and chatting. He guided Buck over toward the mission to get out of the sun for a few minutes.

A community well was situated in the center of the village with a watering trough for animals. He led Buck over to the leaky wooden trough and let him drink. He reached into the cool water, scooped up a handful, and splashed it on his face. He wiped his face with his bandanna, then drew a bucket full from the circular stone basin and took a long drink.

The old adobe mission appeared to be in good condition considering its age. The grounds around the building were weedless, and he saw three clay flowerpots with blooming red flowers near the entrance. The outside walls showed signs that they had been whitewashed sometime in the past few months.

As he drank his fill from the well, a man dressed in a long brown robe approached him from the mission.

"Good afternoon," the man said. "Welcome to the village of Saint Anthony. I'm Father Matthew."

"Good afternoon, Father. I just stopped by for a breather."

"You're most welcome. We don't often get visitors here at Saint Anthony's."

Father Matthew was a heavyset Anglo, broad in the shoulders and wide around the waist. His face was a match for his body, round and full. His long brown hair hung down in wavy strands past the collar of his robe.

"You have a real nice place here, Father."

"Thank you. Many of the men and women in the community took it upon themselves to care for the mission over the years when it was unoccupied. I came here eighteen months ago from San Antonio to assist in its renewal."

"I'm surprised to see an active mission so far removed from the populated areas."

"There are a few missions like our small Saint Anthony's Mission that serve as religious outposts. We teach and minister in a small environment. This mission thrived until it was raided and ransacked by border bandits a few years ago—about twelve years ago, if my memory serves. After that, its place in the community diminished."

"It looks like you have things progressing well, Father. I'm going to rest for a bit longer then I'll be moving on."

Clint tied Buck to a tree and strolled around the mission grounds. At the rear of the adobe structure he saw a woman making rapid strokes with a hoe as she worked in a small garden. The woman noticed him approaching and turned her back to him. He walked around the building where he found an open door at the rear. He stuck his head in and looked around. Seven white candles in a gold candlestick holder provided enough light for him to see the interior. But before he could look around further he was startled by someone speaking behind him.

"It is a beautiful candlestick holder, do you not think, *senor?*"

The speaker was the woman he had seen in the garden. She was carrying a basket of vegetables in the crook of her arm. She was a short, thin, dark-skinned woman with sharp facial features that somehow didn't go with her soft voice.

"Yes, it's beautiful. I'm not much of a religious person, but I'm surprised to see such a magnificent object in a small mission such as this. Did Father Matthew bring it with him?"

"Oh, no. It just appeared on the altar one day a few years ago. This candlestick holder and several other religious objects were stolen by bandits from the south many years ago. But they began to reappear. First, the candlestick holder and a golden cross covered with jewels. Then a gold cup, then another gold cup. Prayers are a wonderful thing, are they not, *senor*?"

"Juanita," someone said from the front of the church. "Let's not bother our guest. He might prefer to meditate in solitude in the house of our Lord."

The woman beat a hasty retreat out the door without looking back.

"She wasn't bothering me, Father. She was just showing me the beautiful candlestick holder. She said it just appeared a few years ago because of their prayers."

"Yes, the people here are very naive when it comes to religious beliefs, sometimes too much so I fear. This candlestick holder and the cups are a good example of that. They were stolen by bandits many years ago, and when they began to reappear, the parishioners believe it was due to their prayers."

"You don't believe that?"

"Oh, I believe in prayer, sir. But in this case, it's possible the religious objects were returned by one of the villagers who began to feel guilty about the theft and brought them back. I'm not saying that's what happened, but I am saying it's a possibility."

Clint smiled. "Maybe in answer to Juanita's prayers?"

Father Matthew shrugged his shoulders. "Maybe, who knows?"

CHAPTER FIFTEEN

Clint had been on the road for over an hour after he left Saint Anthony's Mission when he spotted a weatherworn sign that read Holliday Ranch. It had a black arrow pointing toward the low hills to the west. Clint kneed Buck in that direction. He was doubtful that the shooting incident involving the rancher and Ed Wilhoit's death were connected, but he felt a need to know for certain.

It was mid afternoon when he approached the ranch house. He stopped under an arched gateway with *Welcome to the Holliday Ranch* burned into the wood. Below him, down a slight slope, sat a spacious two-story stone-and-timber house within a grove of tall oak trees. A sturdy timber barn, twice the size of the main house, stood off to the right, along with a wide rectangular bunkhouse. A dozen or more horses pranced around in a corral that must have been at least one hundred yards square. The clanging of hammer against anvil rang out from a lean-to shelter at the side of the barn. His initial impression was that the Holliday Ranch was a well-maintained, prosperous operation.

Just the kind of place I want.

He adjusted his hat and started moving Buck toward the house. Buck had taken no more than two steps when a bullet ricocheted off the sign support and whizzed over Clint's head. He dived off Buck and hit the hard ground with a thud. He scrambled to his knees and found cover behind a mound of dirt. He had his gun at the ready.

"You up there," someone shouted from the front of the house. "Who are you, and what do you want?"

He spat out a mouthful of dust and wiped the dirt from his eyes. He remained still, not wanting to invite another shot. He waited.

The person shouted again. "Mister, who are you, and what do you want? Strangers aren't wanted around here. You'd better speak up, or I'm going to send some more lead your way."

That's a woman shooting at me!

He lay there trying to decide what to do. It didn't seem he had much of a choice. It didn't seem sensible for him to shoot back at a woman, no matter of the circumstances. So he holstered his gun, stood, and held his hands up high to show he was unarmed.

"Walk on down here, but be slow about it. I've got a gun aimed right at your gullet."

Clint walked down the entranceway as instructed. The woman was standing on the porch concealed behind one of the porch supports. She stepped out as he got closer, but never lowered the rifle. When he got within thirty yards of the house, a man came out the door hobbling on a crutch.

The man grabbed the rifle out of the woman's hands. "What are you doing?" the man shouted. "That's not the way we welcome visitors around here."

Another man came around the corner of the house holding a Winchester in his hands. Riders came rushing into the yard from all directions, each with a gun pointed at Clint. He had been in precarious positions before, but he never recalled being surrounded with so many guns pointed at him—and him with his gun hand empty. The riders closed in, encircling him.

The man with the Winchester limped over and took the Colt from Clint's holster, then motioned him toward the porch. "Git going, stranger."

"Here, Gimpy," the man with the crutches said. "Take this rifle and hide it where she can't get to it."

Clint took a chance and lowered his hands when he reached the porch. "I'm not here to cause you any trouble," he said. "I came here to speak with Mister Holliday."

"I'm Justus Holliday," the man with the crutch said. "And I want you to know this is *not* how we welcome people to our ranch." He turned toward the young woman and frowned. "This is my daughter, Calico. She gets a little rambunctious sometimes and forgets her manners."

Clint hadn't taken a good look at the woman until then, and was surprised at what he saw. She was tall, around five feet ten inches, he guessed, with a trim body, and long blonde hair pulled back and tied with a red ribbon. She had the bluest eyes he had ever seen, and a western tanned face. She wore a tan leather riding skirt, a red-and-white-checkered shirt, and gleaming black boots. A handsome lass to be sure.

And there's something else about her. What is it?

Justus Holliday waved a hand at his cowpunchers. "Go on about your business, men. I think this was all a big misunderstanding."

To Clint he said, "Come on into the house and tell me why you wanted to talk to me."

The front room was spacious and open, well lighted with half a dozen handmade chairs of excellent craftsmanship scattered around. An eight-foot-wide floor-to-ceiling stone fireplace dominated one side wall, with handcrafted bookcases on either side holding hundreds of books. The usual array of antlers hung on the other varnished wood walls. The room had a hominess that Clint appreciated.

Holliday walked over to the largest chair in the room and,

with care, lowered himself down onto a fluffy, padded cushion. He laid the crutch across his lap as he caught his breath. "Whew, I'll be glad to rid myself of this kindling."

The pretty lass took a chair beside her father. Clint sat down in a sturdy, cane-bottomed chair across from him.

"Now, if you're looking for a job, that might be possible, but my foreman, Joe Peterson, handles that chore for the ranch these days. He's always on the lookout for good punchers. But being quite honest with you, you don't have the look of a cowpuncher."

"No, Mister Holliday, I'm not looking for a job on your ranch. My name is Clint Ramsay. I came to San Reale to see Sheriff Ed Wilhoit at his request. Upon arriving, I learned that Ed had been killed by a bushwhacker the day before I arrived. Then later, I learned that you had also been shot by a bushwhacker. I rode out here to see if there might be any connection between the two shootings."

"Clint Ramsay," Holliday said. "You were once a Ranger, I believe."

Holliday looked over at his daughter and said, "Calico, you tried to shoot a Ranger. It's a good thing you didn't make him mad."

"How was I to know? He should've made his business known."

Clint smiled as he said, "You didn't give me much of a chance to explain, now did you?"

"Yeah, well, we've already had one run-in with a stranger around here and I wasn't about to take a chance on another one."

"You're forgiven," he said.

Her eyes blazed at him. "I wasn't apologizing, mister, I was explaining."

"But back to my question," Clint said, trying to ignore her

65

obstinacy. "From everything I've heard since I arrived in the area, one shooting is a rarity around here, but three shootings within a few days of each other might not be coincidences."

"Three shootings?" Holliday asked.

Clint told them about his encounter with the bushwhackers on the road into San Reale.

Holliday pursed his lips. "That is troubling. But I don't see how they could be connected to my shooting. Ed and I had very little association with each other over the years, and this is the first time I ever met you. But you're right that three shootings, all from ambushes, is a troubling thought."

"And the dying man's last words were that he and the other bushwhacker were paid fifty dollars each to kill me and my friend."

"See, Dad? I told you things were getting worse around here. All this proves it."

They talked on for a few minutes. Clint kept glancing in Calico's direction, finding it difficult to keep his mind on what her father was saying. She didn't appear to notice his glances.

Justus Holliday turned toward an open doorway and shouted, "Rosita. Come into the parlor please."

A woman appeared in the doorway between the parlor and the cooking area. Clint thought the slim, dark-skinned woman might be a blend of Mexican and Indian heritage. She was tall with a relaxed, regal appearance. Her age? Maybe thirty, forty; who could tell? Her black eyes were sharp and piercing.

"Rosita, bring us some of that tea you make. I think our guest must be thirsty after his long ride. That's the least we can do after his rude welcome." Holliday gave Calico another frown as he spoke.

She didn't appear to notice that glance either.

Rosita dipped her head and said, *"Si, senor."*

The two men talked about ranching for a few minutes, then

Rosita appeared with a tray on which sat a pitcher, three glasses, and an array of cookies. "Have some of this concoction Rosita calls tea. I don't know what goes into it. I just drink it and don't ask any questions."

Clint took a drink. It was sweet, but tangy. He gulped down the remainder, and poured himself another glassful.

"You now have a lifetime friend in Rosita," Holliday said. "Anyone who likes her tea is a friend forever." He held out his hand. "Please help me to my feet, Mister Ramsay. My leg is aching and I need to go lie down for a bit. I'm sorry that I couldn't be of more help to you. But as I said, I just can't see a connection in the shootings."

Clint helped him stand. "Thank you for your time, Mister Holliday. If I learn anything of importance, I'll get word to you."

"Yes, do that. Calico, see Mister Ramsay to the door. And please don't shoot him on the way out."

She stuck out her tongue at her father. "Very funny."

They walked out on the porch. Gimpy had rounded up Buck and had him tied to the hitching post in front of the house. Clint's gun was lying on the saddle. The ranch seemed to have returned to normal after the few minutes of excitement. The blacksmith was clanging away at his anvil, and the corral was surrounded by men shouting insults at a buster who was trying to subdue a sleek black stallion.

"I guess I ought to apologize," Calico said. "It's just that seeing Dad like that, unable to move around, to take care of the ranch, just angers me to no end. I vowed to not let it happen again. So, I'm sorry I took the shots at you."

"As I said before, you're forgiven. You missed."

"Oh, no. I didn't miss. If I had intended to hit you I would have. That's why Dad isn't madder than he is. He knew if I had intended to hit you, I would have. When I pull the trigger, I don't miss."

He smiled at her tenacity. She wasn't going to give an inch. This was some tough gal.

He mounted Buck and rode up the slope away from the ranch house and toward San Reale. He turned in the saddle to have one last look at the ranch. The beautiful lass was still standing on the porch watching him ride away. To his surprise, she raised a hand and waved.

Calico watched the ex-Ranger ride up the slope away from the ranch. *Clint Ramsay.* She had heard tales of him over the years. Gimpy seemed to know all about him and took pleasure in telling her stories of the man. She assumed that he'd embellished most of them, but she never thought she'd meet up with him. She watched him ride away from the ranch, wondering if she would ever see him again.

Gimpy joined her on the porch.

"Do you know who that was?" she asked.

Gimpy nodded. "I knew who he was when he walked up to the house. I've seen him up close on a couple of occasions. He's a real man. That I can say with some certainty."

"He said he came to San Reale because the sheriff asked him to. Do you think he'll stay around to find the sheriff's killer, or be moving on?"

Gimpy squinted at her. "Why are you asking?"

"Oh, just curious, that's all."

"Just curious, huh," he said. "First you take a potshot at him, then you stand on the porch all starry-eyed, and even wave good-bye to him."

"You wipe that bobcat grin off your grizzled old face and mind your own business."

Gimpy walked away cackling like an old mother hen.

But another thought came to her mind also: this ex-Ranger

was a notch or two better-looking than the other men who came to the ranch courting her. All of those she had dismissed out of hand. But this tall, green-eyed man . . . Well . . .

And to think, I shot at him! It would serve me right if he never returned.

Chapter Sixteen

A haze of blue smoke slapped at Clint as he entered the Half-Moon Saloon. He had ridden in from the Holliday Ranch an hour past dark with his throat parched. After downing a drink or two, he planned to look up Harley and fill him in on his day. He stood at the bat-wing doors and scanned the interior. He spotted two tables of cardplayers, and another table with two men conversing over half-filled glasses of beer. Two more men stood at the bar, each with a boot propped on the brass railing. One of the tables with cardplayers caught his attention right off. The men seated there were younger than most of the men in the saloon. They were dressed in dingy, working cowboy outfits, and were more boisterous than the others in the room.

Eyes turned in his direction as he stepped into the saloon, but soon returned to their own business. He walked up to the oak-plank bar and nodded toward the bartender. "Beer," he said, scratching at the itchy growth of black stubble on his cheeks and chin. He glanced at his reflection in the gold-framed mirror that hung behind the bar.

Maybe I should visit Juan again for another bath and shave.

Clint had formulated his long-range plan during the years he had followed dusty trails. He had endured dangers, hardships, and loneliness to get into the position in which he now found himself. His Kansas City bank account had grown to the point that he now had more than enough set aside to buy that ranch he had been dreaming about for years. The old-timers had told

70

him the trick for any hired gun was to settle down before he met someone a little quicker on the draw, or a little truer with his aim. Now past thirty years old, his body had aches and pains that did not disappear as they once did. Like Lucas had said; it was a hard life they had chosen—and one Clint was ready to leave behind.

Just then a high-pitched, whiskey-laden shout shook the saloon. "Hey bartender, bring us a bottle of that rat poison over here."

"Be there in just a minute," the bartender said. "As soon as I get this gentleman his beer."

"I said now. The gentleman can wait."

Clint turned toward the sound. It came from a red-faced kid seated at a table with three other young cardplayers all about his age. He might have been eighteen years old, but he was try-ing to act like he was forty.

The bartender looked from the cowboy to Clint, unsure of what to do next.

"Go ahead, take him the bottle," Clint said with a slight shrug of his shoulders. "I can wait."

The young cowboy heard the remark and swaggered up to the bar and stood a few feet from him. He wore two guns, both slung low and tied down, cocksure of himself in front of an audience and this stranger. He squared his stance, legs wide, his left hand hovering over his gun. "Sure you can wait. You're gonna wait 'cause I said you're gonna wait."

Here we go again.

Myron Welborn, president of Cattlemen's Bank, sat with his back to the wall and watched as Willie Teal approached the tall stranger. "This could get interesting," he said with a grin. "Looks like the Teal kid is out to cut a notch on his gun."

Across from Myron sat Tobin Fletcher, who, like Myron, was

dressed in a black suit with a white shirt and a black string tie. "Does this happen often?" Fletcher asked.

Myron took a cheroot from his vest pocket, bit off the end, and rolled it between his fingers. He wasn't sure which was more entertaining: the looming confrontation between the Teal kid and the stranger, or Fletcher's obvious discomfort at the possibility of gunplay. Fletcher had arrived on the afternoon stage from San Antonio with a business proposition, which the two had discussed back at Myron's office. After growing weary of the talk, Myron had suggested they retire to the Half-Moon for a libation.

"With Willie Teal, yes," Myron answered, as he handed Fletcher one of his cheroots. "About once a month around payday—when he's flush with drinking money. He's the town hothead. Most of the men he confronts know him and let him huff and puff, then back away. But he has run into a couple who didn't back away."

"What happened to them?"

Myron recalled the two incidents, and said, "Teal plugged one in the shoulder, and the other one lost an ear. As yet, he hasn't killed anyone, but it's just a matter of time. He's headed for a tough life unless someone comes along and shows him the error of his ways."

Fletcher took another sip of his beer and nodded toward the unkempt stranger. "What about this man? Will he back away, too?"

"Maybe. Maybe not. One of these days, Teal will pick on the wrong person."

In fact, Myron thought, there was something about the stranger—a clear-eyed and unflinching resolve—that suggested Teal might be about to get an education.

"Do you know the drifter?" Fletcher asked.

"Never laid eyes on him before."

Fletcher struck a lucifer and put it to the cheroot Myron had given him. As he let out the smoke, he reached into his vest pocket and pulled out a gold coin and spun it on the table. "Want to put twenty dollars on it?"

"Sure, why not. At least maybe they'll create a little excitement in this cow town. Your call."

Fletcher waved his hand. "I say the stranger backs down."

Myron heard the drifter's voice again as he faced the kid. Yes, this might get interesting. He toyed with the cheroot as he watched the two men play out their drama.

CHAPTER SEVENTEEN

Clint was tired, thirsty, and in no mood for a fight. "Look, cowboy, you've got your bottle, now go on back to your game and let me be. I've just had a long ride and I'm tired. I don't need all this aggravation."

"Aggravation, is it?" The cowboy eased away from the bar another step. He glanced toward his friends at the card table. "Did you hear that? This gentleman says I'm aggravating him."

There was the sound of forced laughter coming from the table, but the rest of the room was quiet in anticipation of what was about to happen. They had seen it before.

Clint turned away from the bar to face the cowboy. He stood straight, his arms hanging at his sides. Two men who were standing beside him set their glasses on the bar and moved to another part of the room.

Someone in the saloon coughed and Teal went for his gun.

Clint reacted with a coolness based on long experience. He palmed his gun and had it pointed at the cowboy's stomach before the cowboy had cleared leather with his gun. Clint could hear the hush in the crowd as they waited for the gunshot. But he didn't pull the trigger. He held the Colt steady, the hammer still cocked, and the business end pointed at the cowboy's midsection.

After a minute, he broke the silence with a soft-but-forceful statement. "That was just a practice run, cowboy. Now we're going do it for real."

Clint made a show of releasing the hammer on his Colt and dropping the gun back into his holster. He pointed to one of the cowboy's friends at the card table. "You over there. You start counting to three real slow like." He turned his cold stare back at the cowboy standing in front of him. "When your friend over there reaches three, we'll do it for real this time. The fun is over. No more practice. We'll finish what you wanted when you stepped up to the bar and braced me. On the count of three you had better start shooting, understand? Start the count."

The young cowboy began backing away. Sweat beaded above his lip, his left eye twitched. He took another step back. Clint could hear the cowboy's breathing become shallower, more labored, as if he had just finished a footrace.

"Start counting," he said louder, matching the cowboy's retreating steps with steps of his own. "All right, it seems your buddy doesn't know how to count, so I'll do it for him. One."

The cowboy's head began turning left and right. "Somebody stop him, he's going to kill me." His eyes were glazed with fear. "Somebody stop him."

"Two."

The cowboy lifted his hands away from his guns. In a voice filled with terror, he said, "I'm not going to draw on him. It'll be murder if he shoots me. I'm not going to draw."

Clint stopped within arm's reach of the cowboy and stared at him. He motioned to the other cowboys at the table. "You had better come get your friend here, and get him out of town before I change my mind. And you'd better be quick about it, because I'm about to lose my patience."

"He got in here all by hisself," one of them said. "I guess he can get out the same way. He don't need our help." The three cowboys stood and walked out the front door of the saloon.

The cowboy watched as his friends abandoned him, one by one. When he realized that the stranger was going to let him live to see another day, he turned and marched out the door behind them, not looking anyone in the face.

Clint could hear the hushed whispering in the saloon, and could feel the eyes staring at him as the crisis ended.

Why did that fool have to pick today to get drunk?

Tobin Fletcher tapped the ashes off the cheroot and smiled. He then picked up the twenty-dollar gold piece and flipped it to Welborn. "You have a good eye, Myron. Remind me not to wager with you again. That man wasn't intimidated in the least. Your Willie was one lucky man. That stranger isn't your run-of-the-mill cowboy, that's for sure."

"He's different from most of the gunmen I've heard tales about. Allison, Sam Bass, and Hardin; those men would have pulled the trigger on Teal in a heartbeat. Yeah, this one is fast on the draw for sure, but different from them in that regard."

Fletcher leaned back in his chair and toyed with the cheroot. "I wonder what brought a man like that to San Reale. Doesn't it seem a bit strange to you that a man who's that skilled with a gun would just happen to wander into a remote town like this?"

"Gunfighters go where the money is. He might be just passing through, or he might have business with someone in San Reale."

"I wonder who that person might be."

Myron Welborn, president of the Cattlemen's Bank, respected businessman, and a long-standing member of the San Reale Town Council laughed and said, "I hope it's not me he's after."

CHAPTER EIGHTEEN

Myron Welborn arrived at his office in the Cattlemen's Bank at six o'clock the following morning. He sat with a cup of coffee at his elbow while he thumbed through a stack of papers that Tobin Fletcher had left with him. The proposition Fletcher presented to him was one that he'd never expected to see. It could be worth over thirty thousand dollars to him if they came to an agreement. Furthermore, it seemed to be legal and aboveboard. While he'd never been one to be concerned about legalities, Myron still considered caution to be his byword. He hadn't accumulated his modest fortune by going too far beyond the law, but by taking advantage of opportunities as they arose. This was one opportunity that he couldn't let pass.

The door to his office opened two hours later as he was still concentrating on the proposal's language. It was his wife, Siena. She was another of his prized possessions. She could be difficult at times, for sure, but he felt a certain manliness to be seen in company with her. She gave him a sense of status around town that other men envied. She had long black hair that hung past her shoulders and opal-colored eyes that shined. Even now, after all this time, he didn't think he'd ever seen anyone quite so striking. This morning, she was wearing another of Miss Beatrice's expensive creations.

He looked at her with pride as she entered the office. She was twenty-one years his junior, and he had no delusions as to why she had agreed to marry him, but it didn't matter to him.

She was his now.

Welborn knew Siena was an ambitious young woman who was tired of being tied down to a humdrum life in a hot, dusty, boring Texas cow town. Paris, London, and Venice; those were the cities of her dreams. How often had she told him the wind and sagebrush of Texas could go to Hades as far as she was concerned? She wanted the sparkling city lights, the glamorous balls, and a host of servants always at her side. The reality here was something much different. Here she was, stuck in backwater San Reale, Texas, married to a man she once, in a screaming fit of anger, called "a fifty-three-year-old, overweight, nearsighted, money-grubbing oaf."

Myron had met her during a bankers' meeting in Austin. He and a few of his banking cronies had been having a high time at a private club called The Tumbleweed, following a day of contentious arguing over state banking regulations. Siena had strutted by their table on the arm of a young politician. Myron had been captivated by her from that first glance. As the night progressed, he found that he couldn't take his eyes off her. Her escort, being a politician through and through, had begun making the rounds visiting tables and shaking hands, leaving Siena alone at their table.

Myron summoned up his courage and approached her. She had ignored him at first, but before the night was over, she had agreed to meet him at The Tumbleweed the following night. He wasn't to be denied. He waved fists full of money in her face for the remainder of the week. His money, his promises, and her fantasy-filled ambitions, soon persuaded her to return to San Reale with him as Mrs. Myron Welborn. Now she was his for better or for worse.

"And to what do I owe this pleasure?" he said, walking around his desk. He leaned toward her to kiss her, but she tilted her head to the side and presented her cheek for a quick peck. He returned to his chair, angry at her rebuff, but sensible enough to remain silent.

She sat down on the edge of his desk and crossed her legs in a provocative pose, letting one foot caress his leg. She burst out laughing at his discomfort. "Does dear ol' Annie over at the Half-Moon make you blush like that? I'll bet with all her experience, she can light you up like a Christmas candle."

Welborn shoved her foot away. "For God's sake, Siena, did you come over here to start that argument all over again? I told you Annie was a thing of the past."

"We'll discuss that at another time, dear. Now I have something to tell you. Did you hear about the incident over at the Half-Moon?"

"You mean the one between Willie Teal and that cowboy?"

"Yes, that's the one."

"Well, what about it?" he said. There was nothing for him to gain by letting her know that he was a witness to it. The fact he was at the Half-Moon was something she didn't need to know. "It's about time somebody put that hothead in his place."

She reached out and straightened his string tie as she spoke. "That cowboy, as you call him, is no ordinary cowboy. In fact, he's a most extraordinary man, from what I can gather from all the talk around town. He has already shot one man and backed down Willie Teal, all in a couple of days. And he just might be here to settle some debts for a few of your old customers."

He pushed her hands away. "What do you mean? What are you talking about?"

"Have you ever heard of the Underwood Detective Agency?"

"Of course. Everyone west of the Mississippi has heard of Underwood. What's that got to do with anything?"

"That cowboy in the Half-Moon was none other than an Underwood detective named Clint Ramsay."

That got his attention. "Are you sure of that?" The image of the man in the saloon came to mind, as did his lightning-quick draw. Welborn could well believe that he was no ordinary cowhand—but an Underwood man—and Clint Ramsay, at that. He'd heard stories of the man when he had been with the Rangers. Ramsay was hell on wheels, if you could believe the stories that had been told about him.

"That's the word around town," she said. "And I doubt an Underwood detective would be in San Reale for the scenery."

Welborn stood and began pacing the office, his hands clasped behind his back. He walked to the side window in his office and stared out into the alley. He then looked back at Siena. Did she know more than she was telling?

Siena walked over and placed her hands on the back of his neck and massaged it. "I suggest you find a way to handle this Ramsay fellow on your own before he can ask too many questions, or your little empire might come crumbling down around your cute little ears."

He turned and faced her. She leaned in and kissed him hard on the lips, then patted him on the cheek. "That's what I suggest you do, dear. Find a gunman of your own and solve the problem before he can ruin us."

She then sauntered out of the bank with Myron staring at her.

Where am I going to find a gunman able to handle a man like Clint Ramsay?

CHAPTER NINETEEN

Clint met Harley at Martha Ann's for one of Louise's breakfast specials. The sun was well up in the sky, but he had enjoyed the feather mattress so much, that he'd been reluctant to leave it. Harley had to pound on the door of his room to wake him. They exchanged information over a platter of wheat cakes and eggs in the boardinghouse dining room. He told Harley about his run-in with the young cowboy, Saint Anthony's Mission, Father Matthew, and his visit to the Holliday Ranch.

He never mentioned the beautiful lass who had taken a shot at him.

Harley had little to add to their knowledge except gossip and rumors. The one rumor that held any promise was of an abandoned homestead outside of town that cowboys said had come to life again with a lot of comings and goings. He said the redheaded woman had left the Sundown Saloon just one time as far as he could tell. She rode in a buckboard down to the mercantile and came out with two boxes of groceries. Other than that, she stayed inside the saloon.

"I did hear the gossip going around that new Sheriff Elder was talking big," Harley said. "Elder has bragged around town that he'd given us two more days to leave town, or that he was going to see that we left."

"That arrogant fool is going to get himself shot before he has a chance to polish his badge."

"Be a waste of good lead."

Clint put his elbows on the table and tepeed his hands in front of him. "None of this makes a lot of sense to me. I can't see a connection between the shooting of Ed and Justus Holliday, or what this country has to offer anyone who's out to hit a big jackpot." He ran his hands through his hair and leaned back in his chair. "I just can't figure it out."

"Me neither," said Harley. "But I wouldn't put it past that coyote of a deputy to shoot somebody from behind a tree. That seems more likely than anything else we've found."

"That might explain Ed's death, but it still doesn't explain why Ed sent for us, or why we were ambushed. If it was just Elder, Ed could've handled him without anyone's help. No, there's something else that Ed knew that got him killed."

About that time, a young boy ran into the dining room and looked around. He spotted Clint and hurried over to his table. The boy threw down a piece of paper and ran out again. Clint reached out a hand toward the boy's back in a futile effort to grab his arm.

"Wait, wait. Come back," he shouted, but the boy disappeared around the corner and was gone. He picked up the piece of paper, which was folded over on itself twice, and opened it. He read the note, then read it a second time.

"You goin' to share it with me?" Harley asked.

He handed the note across the table. "It's from Marva. It looks like that reward talk started her to thinking. She's waiting out behind the boardinghouse and wants to talk to me."

"Could be a trick, you know? How fer do you trust her?"

"I don't know her well enough to either trust her or not trust her. If we have even a slight chance of her shedding some light on this situation, I don't think I can pass up having another conversation with her."

Clint walked through the kitchen to the rear of the boarding-house. He stood on the back porch and looked around for

Marva. After a moment, he saw her standing near the corner of the adjacent building. He walked toward her.

She grabbed him by the arm and pulled him into the shadows. "Quick, let's get this over before I'm seen by somebody."

"I got your note. What do you want to tell me?"

"First I want the money, then I'll tell you how you can catch a man who might have killed Ed."

"Sorry, Marva, it doesn't work that way. You get the money when we get the man. And you said 'might have killed Ed.' "

"I won't say another word until I see the money. If you want him, get me the money today. I don't want any excuses."

Clint played a bluff and turned to leave. She grabbed his arm again and pulled him back. "All right, all right. Give me half of the reward money now, then when you catch him, I get the other half. Is that a deal?"

"I don't carry that kind of money with me. It would take several days for me to make arrangements for an amount of money that large. You'll just have to trust me. If your information leads to the capture of Ed's killer, I'll see that you get the reward. That's the best I can do."

She bit on her lower lip, thinking about it. "If I tell you enough to catch him, then, I'll get the reward money, right?"

"Let's hear your information. I'm not convinced that you know."

She wet her lips and looked around. "I'm to meet a man at Pinhead's place out by the stage depot after dark tonight. I'm sure he's the man you're looking for." She then ran down the alleyway and out of sight.

CHAPTER TWENTY

Myron Welborn sat at a table at the rear of the Half-Moon Saloon staring at a glass of whiskey. His mind was reeling with what Siena had told him: Clint Ramsay, an Underwood detective, was here in San Reale. Welborn was not a heavy drinker as a rule. He confined his drinking to an occasional glass of whiskey when it was related to a business deal; however, today was different. His life's work, his lifelong ambitions, were now in jeopardy. He was on his third drink with the bottle a little more than half full sitting there in front of him. The more he thought about it, and the more whiskey he consumed, the more convinced he became that Ramsay had been sent here to settle an old score for one of the many people he had dealt with in the past.

People I have cheated.

But which one? There were too many for him to recall. Still, he was certain that one of his former customers had hired Ramsay to right a past wrong. He was sure of it. Then it struck him; the proposition that Tobin Fletcher had brought him involved twelve thousand acres to the northeast of San Reale that Myron now owned. He had gained ownership of the property as a result of a foreclosure on Able Trimble's mortgaged ranch.

Tobin Fletcher was a representative of the Great Western Railroad Company, a company interested in running a line to San Reale to handle the local cattle market. The preliminary route they had drawn up would take the tracks straight through the former Trimble spread. Myron stood to make a small fortune if the deal went through.

That was it. It had to be Able Trimble.

He took another drink, closed his eyes and tried to remember Trimble. It hadn't taken but one meeting at the bank for Myron to figure out that Trimble was an illiterate rancher who knew nothing about mortgages, foreclosures, or banking protocol. Easy pickings. But Trimble had turned out to be a hard-working man who fought through long droughts, hard winters, and a thousand others things that Texas ranchers faced. He had held on from year to year by sheer will and hard work—until Myron, seeing no other way to gain control of the ranch, began tinkering with his account.

While Trimble hadn't understood the intricacies of banking, he did understand when he was being cheated. When Sheriff Ed Wilhoit served the foreclosure papers on Trimble, and explained what it all meant, Trimble packed his belongings in a wagon and rode toward San Reale and the Cattlemen's Bank.

Welborn remembered it well. The sun had passed midday when Trimble had stopped his wagon in front of the bank. He entered with his double-barreled shotgun in his hands, and a pocketful of shells. He nodded at the teller and told the young man to lie down on the floor and to stay there. Welborn watched from the doorway of his office as Trimble thumbed back the hammers on the double-barreled shotgun and began blasting away. Welborn had jumped behind his desk as the shooting started, then continued, blast after blast. When the shooting stopped, Trimble had demolished the interior of the bank from top to bottom. Paper money from the teller trays covered the floor, the furniture and desks had been splintered, and all the glass in the building had been shattered.

Ed Wilhoit said later that he had found seventeen empty shotgun shells scattered around the bank when Trimble had finished shooting. After wrecking the bank, Trimble took his empty shotgun back to the wagon and waited for the sheriff to appear.

"It's got to be Trimble," Myron said. "It has to be."

He was aware that Trimble had been released from prison less than a year ago. *Now he has heard about the railroad.* Myron grabbed the whiskey glass and gulped down the drink, then poured another one. He had seen the Underwood man up close, here in this very saloon. He had seen him in action. It was no dream. Clint Ramsay was here to get him for the Trimble swindle.

What am I going to do? Ramsay came here to expose me—to ruin me. Maybe even kill me!

He looked down at his hands. They were shaking. But he knew he had one bargaining chip at his disposal if push came to shove. On the day Ed Wilhoit had been killed, Myron was riding north of the town looking over a piece of property. He heard rifle shots, and being cautious, he had ducked into a grove of trees. That's when Jake Polk had raced past him, away from the spot where Wilhoit was found dead a little later. He knew it was Polk who had shot Wilhoit, but had said nothing about it. After all, Polk had always been a good customer and maintained a considerable amount of money in his account.

"Hey, Myron," Annie Keeler said, as she strolled over to his table. "What's the matter? Why are you crying in your beer?"

Myron looked up at her then checked the saloon for onlookers. The last thing he needed was some loudmouth telling Siena about this. "I told you not to speak to me in here."

"I'll go up to my room," she said, smiling. "You can join me there if you want to. I believe you know the way."

He watched her walk away, trying to resist the temptation to join her. But the alcohol he'd consumed gave him the courage to follow her. He downed the remaining whiskey from the glass and walked up the stairs to her room.

Annie sat on the bed waiting for him, her legs crossed, smoking a thin cigarillo. She had changed into a fluffy green robe. She stood, walked over to him, and put her arms around his neck. "I thought you would show up. Want to get right down to business like in the old days? It's been a long time."

He reached up and removed her hands. "I can't, Annie," he said. "I've got a real problem I have to take care of, and I've got to think it out." He sat down on the edge of the bed with his head buried in his hands. "It's making me crazy."

"Can't pretty little Siena help you?" Annie walked over to a table and crushed out her cigarillo in a pewter dish. She turned and said, "Don't you talk to her about your problems like you used to talk to me? You once told me all your little secrets."

She was right, except for one important point; he didn't tell her *all* of his little secrets. Still, for some reason, he had always trusted Annie. He took his hands from his face and began waving them around as he told her about Clint Ramsay, leaving out the Trimble motive. He didn't trust her, or anyone else, knowing about that deal.

"This Underwood detective has been brought here by someone to investigate me, and I don't know how to stop him. It's making me crazy."

Annie was a slender, attractive brunette with a small, heart-shaped face. Myron had been attracted to her from the first moment he'd met her, even though he well knew how she made her living. He had visited her often in the years before his marriage to Siena, and had continued his visits afterwards, although not as often.

"Think about it for a minute, Myron. This Ramsay fellow had a run-in with Willie Teal in front of half the town. Everyone is talking about it. A man of your persuasive ability should be able to get Willie to help you if you give him the proper incentive."

She lifted her hand and rubbed her index finger with her thumb. "That's incentive enough for most men. And I'll bet you a dollar to a dime, Willie is already trying to think of a way to get even with Ramsay. Both of you can solve your problems at the same time."

Myron looked up at her with a startled expression on his face. Willie's old man, Ernest Teal, was deep in debt to him, with a hefty ranch mortgage and a couple of smaller loans. He had lent Teal more money against that property than he would have under normal circumstances. The Teal ranch bordered another piece of property Myron owned, and there was little chance that Teal could make the inflated mortgage payment. He would then force a foreclosure and gain legal ownership of the Teal land. However, if Willie could get rid of Ramsay for him, then he might get rid of Ernest's debt, or at least a part of it.

And even better, everyone in town knew that Ramsay had backed Willie down in the saloon, so if the younger Teal retaliated and killed Ramsay, it wouldn't surprise anyone. Myron would be in the clear.

He stood and dropped Fletcher's twenty-dollar coin on her table. "Annie, you may have saved my life."

He left Annie's room whistling, but of more importance, he left with a plan.

CHAPTER TWENTY-ONE

Jake Polk dismounted at the rear of Pinhead's cabin for his regular visit with Marva. He was thirty minutes ahead of time, as was his practice. It was after his appointment to the city council that he had told her to find them another place to get together. A certain amount of decorum was expected of a councilman. He had not explained this to Marva, but neither did Marva question his reasons. He knew as long as he kept her flush with money, she was open to anything he suggested.

She had worked out a deal with a Sundown bartender for them to use his cabin. The two of them had begun meeting at the cabin in the afternoon, before the Sundown Saloon's night-time crowd arrived. Jake hadn't been all that pleased with the meeting place. It was trashy and unkempt, but it would do for their purposes. His stay in this town wasn't to be long in duration anyway, if things went as he'd planned. Jake guessed he could endure a little discomfort every now and then.

Jake always approached from the tree side of the cabin, avoiding the main road. He felt somewhat safe, but he took no chances, always arriving before the set time just in case he was wrong. Marva's one-horse buggy was tied to a bush, and the nag was nibbling on the sparse grass that grew around the old cabin. He laid his hand on the butt of his gun and dismounted, still wary of his surroundings. She'd never been early before, always a few minutes late. He didn't like unexplained changes in routine.

As he neared the rear door, it flew open, and Marva stood there, dressed in a low-cut red dress with sparkling bangles hanging around her waistline. He'd noticed that she had always made it a point to dress in a manner that revealed her most prominent assets. That little habit had appealed to him and kept him returning to her.

"Come on in, Jake."

He walked through the doorway over to the tall redhead and threw his arms around her waist. He kissed her, then backed away a step to look at her. She was pretty enough, considering that she was beginning to show her age. And the wear and tear of her chosen profession had given her a hardened appearance. While she wasn't in the same league as some of the other women in his past, she had been a pleasant-enough diversion while he and Bobby put the finishing touches on their plan.

One other woman he'd seen in San Reale had caught his attention as well: The banker's wife. But he'd made a point to keep away from her until this job was finished. After that, well, he would see what happened then.

"Jake," Marva said, lowering her head. "I need some money."

"Why, sure." He reached into his pocket and pulled out a fistful of greenbacks. "Here's about twenty dollars," he said, holding out the money toward her. "Take all you want. There's more where this came from."

She slapped at his hand, knocking the money to the floor. "I'm talking about real money. I found out something that you might be interested in knowing. It ought to be worth five hundred dollars at least."

Polk remained still, but inside he was seething. He waited to see what this saloon woman was after, and he thought he knew. What she didn't know was the kind of man she was dealing with.

"So you know something that's worth five hundred dollars to me?"

"I do. How about it?"

"What if I don't think it's worth five hundred dollars? What then?"

"It's worth it, believe me."

He reached in his pocket and pulled out a leather wallet. He riffled through it and then laid five hundred dollars on the table. "Let's hear it."

Marva grabbed at it, but Jake was quicker, and took her by the arm. "Come on, Marva, let's hear this important information."

Chapter Twenty-Two

Clint believed it would be safer and less intrusive for him and Harley to walk to Pinhead's cabin rather than ride their horses. He figured it would take the two of them ten to fifteen minutes to reach the cabin by taking the backstreets and alleyways to keep out of sight of the townsfolk.

When they reached the rear of the stage depot, they saw the small cabin a hundred yards away, set in a thick grove of willows and cottonwoods. The front of the cabin faced the main road into San Reale. At the rear, there was a narrow gap in the woods that led to what Clint assumed was a creek, or a small stream. From where he now stood at the edge of the stage depot corral, he could see both the front and rear entrances to the cabin.

Harley stepped out from the depot to get a better view, then made a quick jump back into the shadows. "There's a buggy tied down at the rear of the cabin. Appears to be the same one that Marva used when she went to the mercantile yesterday."

"Hmmm," said Clint. "I wonder what she's up to. She said it would be after dark before she met this man."

"She could be with somebody else. She's a businesswoman of sorts, you know."

"I don't see any horses, or another buggy."

Harley laid a hand on Clint's arm and said, "I'm going to ease round to the back of the cabin and take a look-see. If you hear a call, you might want to join me."

Clint waited for several minutes then heard the cooing sound

92

of a dove coming from the trees behind the cabin. Harley had discovered something.

CHAPTER TWENTY-THREE

Jake Polk was getting angrier by the minute as he stood in front of Marva, who had her hands on her hips and a defiant look on her face. She had been drinking some courage, he thought, as the pungent odor of cheap whiskey drifted toward him.

"Go on, Marva. Tell me all about this expensive information you have."

She raised a hand to her hair and patted at it in a nervous kind of way, then looked down at the floor. "Well . . . a man . . . one of the Underwood detectives named Ramsay, came to see me about Ed Wilhoit. He wanted to know what I knew about Ed's death, since we were together a lot. I didn't tell him a thing, but he offered me a thousand dollars if I would tell him who killed Ed."

"And what did you say?"

"Nothing. I didn't say nothing."

"But you think it was me who killed the sheriff. Is that what you think, Marva?"

"I don't know. Maybe not you, but I know you've got some mean men at your disposal who would shoot Ed in a heartbeat. It's possible. I know how you ran off those other men who wanted to start up freight outfits in town."

Jake put his hands on Marva's shoulders and massaged them. "Come on, Marva. What did you say to Ramsay?" His hands moved off her shoulders to her neck. "Did you tell him my name?"

He could see the fear rising in her eyes as she tried to back away from him, but his fingers dug deeper into her soft flesh. He smiled when he saw her realization of the terrible mistake she had made.

"What did you say, Marva? What did you say to Ramsay?"

"Nothing, I promise. I said nothing. It's . . . it's just . . . well . . . I thought if you gave me some money, I could leave this town for good. Maybe me and you together. Yes, that's what we can do, leave together. How about it?"

Polk smiled as he tightened his hands around her neck. She grabbed his wrists and tried to free herself from his grasp. She tried to scream, but it came out as a whisper, because his hands were too tight around her neck.

"Listen, Jake, I set him up for you," she whispered. "You can get him, today. I set him up for you."

He relaxed his hands. "You did what?"

Marva rubbed her neck where his fingers had dug in. "I set him up for you. That's worth something to you isn't it? Maybe two hundred dollars?"

"Start talking, Marva. How did you set him up?"

"I told him I was going to meet a man here after dark who might know something about the sheriff's death. Now that's worth two hundred dollars. You can get him easy here, and you won't have to worry about him anymore."

But Jake's rage was still simmering inside. He grabbed her around the neck again. "Yes, that's good, Marva, and it might work like you say. But your real purpose in coming out here was to blackmail me wasn't it? That's not a nice thing for a classy whore like you to be doing."

He began squeezing his hands tighter and tighter. He heard a gurgle, saw her eyes roll back in her head and felt her go limp. He released her and she fell to the floor with a hard crash.

He went to the rear door, cracked it open, and peered

through. Clint Ramsay wouldn't wait until dark to approach the cabin. In fact, he could be out there at this very moment, getting himself into position. He sat down and ran the situation through his mind. He went to the door once again and looked out. He couldn't see any movement, nor did he expect to see any. Clint Ramsay was not your local bumbling sheriff.

Polk backed away from the door and looked around the cabin. There was a window on the tree side of the cabin, which gave him an idea. He went over to the jalousie window and tried to raise it, but it wouldn't budge. It was stuck closed. He pounded at it around the edges, then tried again. With some effort the window creaked and broke loose.

It might work; it just might work.

He pulled out a pouch of tobacco and rolled himself a smoke. He put a match to it, then tossed the flaming match onto a pile of trash that had accumulated in the corner of the cabin. He rushed to the window as the flames erupted behind him. He kept a close eye on the fire as it spread. When it got close enough to him that he could feel the searing heat, he lifted the window. He stuck his head out of the opening and searched the area that lay ahead of him. He was certain he could reach the trees and his horse in a matter of seconds without being spotted. He positioned himself to make the jump from the window. Looking back at the fire, he saw the cabin was becoming engulfed with flames, so he jumped and ran toward the trees. His horse was jumping and bucking as the crackling fire alarmed him. Polk mounted the horse and moved farther into the shelter of the thick grove of trees. A few moments later, just as he had suspected, he saw two men running toward the burning cabin.

"Too bad you won't get to enjoy that thousand dollars, Marva," he said, as he rode away from the burning cabin.

Chapter Twenty-Four

Clint first saw smoke coming from under the eaves of the cabin. Then, in a matter of minutes, the whole place was ablaze. "Quick, Harley," he shouted. "If Marva is in there, we have to get her out."

He ran from the trees toward the cabin, with Harley close at his heels. The flames and the heat were too intense for either of them to get close. All they could do was to back away and watch as the ramshackle cabin blazed.

"Maybe I was wrong," Harley said. "Maybe it wasn't her buckboard."

A throng of townspeople came thundering up the road toward them carrying buckets. They established a bucket brigade from the stream behind the cabin and began throwing water on the fire in a futile effort to put it out. Soon the cabin was nothing more than a pile of smoldering ashes. Several men walked around the surrounding area putting out small grass fires before they spread to the stage depot. Others stood around in groups of two and three, pointing and chatting.

Clint stood several yards from the fire with his hat in his hands. His face was red from the heat of the fire. Harley was squatted on his haunches picking at a few weeds.

"Marva was working both ends against the middle," Clint said. "She was playing a dangerous game and it came back and bit her. I suppose we'll find her somewhere in those ashes."

Harley nodded. "I 'spect so."

Clint walked closer to what remained of the old cabin as he felt the heat beginning to diminish. A spiral of black smoke continued to rise from the ashes, but the flames had pretty much died out. He began kicking at the hot ashes at the edge of the foundation. He stopped when he heard someone yelling behind him.

Sam Elder was taking long strides toward him. "Get away from that cabin," he shouted. "What are you doing here? This is none of your concern."

Clint waved his hands at the other men who had congregated. "We just came out with everyone else to see what was going on, Sheriff. That's all."

"Well, you've seen it, now back away."

A man wearing a greasy white apron walked up to them, stuck his nose in the air and said, "Smells like burnt flesh."

"I wonder if there could have been someone in there, Sheriff," Clint said. He walked over to the tree line and returned to the ashes with a thick branch about five feet long. He began kicking and stirring the ashes with the stick. He kicked away the charred, glowing timbers of what were once roof rafters, then called for Elder. He had uncovered a body. Like the rest of the old cabin, it was charred and beyond recognition.

"Now who that could be?" Elder said. He pointed at a man over near the stream. "There's Pinhead over there, so it can't be him."

Others walked over to see what they had discovered.

Clint bent over the body and brushed away the ashes from an object he had seen once before. He lifted it out of the hot coals with the end of the branch. He held the object out in front of him. "It wasn't a man, Sheriff. It's Marva from the Sundown Saloon. I saw her wearing this necklace around her neck when I spoke with her."

"What in tarnation was she doing out here?" Elder asked. He

was silent for a moment, then added, "Well, I guess I know what she was doing out here. I just don't know who she was doing it with."

"I'm sure you will figure it out, Sheriff," Clint said, as he and Harley walked back toward the town.

Chapter Twenty-Five

Myron Welborn had beads of sweat forming on his forehead as he paced in his office, speculating on what-ifs. What if he was wrong and Ramsay was not after him? What if it was Siena who had sent for Ramsay to get rid of him so she could take all of his money and leave this town? What if he offered Ramsay money to leave him alone? What if . . . what if . . .

The knock at the rear door of his office startled him out of his reverie. He stopped his pacing, wiped his forehead with his handkerchief, and glanced at the clock that hung on the office wall: 4:30 p.m. That was the time he had summoned Willie Teal to his office. Myron looked at his hands. They were trembling. He pulled opened his desk drawer and took out the bottle of whiskey he kept around for special customers. He pulled the cork from the bottle and took a giant swallow and replaced it in the drawer. He took a deep breath then walked to the rear door and opened it. Standing in the dim light of the office lantern was Willie Teal.

Willie had a drawn, washed-out look about him. His eyes were red-rimmed, his hair long, stringy, and greasy. Even at his young age, he had the look of someone who was years older. Myron guessed coming face-to-face with death could do that to a person.

"Come in, Willie, come in," he said, with more fervor than he felt. "I'm so glad you could join me. Can I get you a drink? I have some top-notch bourbon, or maybe coffee if you prefer?"

Willie stared back at him, not responding to his offer of a drink, or showing any apparent interest in him, or his bank. Myron's uneasiness increased as he watched Willie's fingers roll back and forth over the butt of his holstered gun.

Am I making a deal with the devil?

The banker hesitated for a moment, then got to the matter at hand. "Willie, I have a proposition to make to you that I think can be of great benefit to both of us." Myron motioned for him to take a seat beside him. "Let me show you a few things."

Myron opened a file folder and pulled out a sheaf of papers. He placed them in front of Willie. "This is the mortgage on your father's ranch." He pointed to a figure at the bottom of the page. "See that number, Willie? That's four thousand, seven hundred and thirty-eight dollars." He then pointed to a paragraph below the number. "See that date? That's three months and sixteen days from now."

Willie looked at Welborn. "So?"

"Do you think your father has four thousand, seven hundred and thirty-eight dollars?" He then pulled out another folder and went through the same spiel, then another. "If we add up all the money your father owes the Cattlemen's Bank, it would be close to six thousand dollars. I have my doubts that your father has six thousand dollars, or can get his hands on that much money in three months. What do you think?"

Willie Teal squirmed in his seat. "I don't know how much money he's got. I ain't never asked, and he ain't never said. Now, why're you telling me all this? Why did you send for me?"

Myron felt his confidence growing. "It's very simple, what I have in mind, Willie. You do something for me, and I do something for you—or in this case, you *and* your father. And there might even be something extra in it for you when all is said and done. That is, if it's done right, with the right outcome."

"What do you want me to do? Out with it, banker, and be

quick about it."

Myron Welborn smiled and told Willie what he wanted him to do.

CHAPTER TWENTY-SIX

Jake Polk and Anse Hocker sat in the back room of the freight warehouse. Polk tipped up the bottle of cheap whiskey that Hocker preferred and took a huge swallow. His face twisted into an ugly snarl as he told Hocker about Marva's double-dealing.

"That . . . She nearly got me killed, that . . ."

He took another swallow of the whiskey, then threw the empty bottle against the rear wall.

"Anse," he said. "We've gotta get rid of this Ramsay character. He's going to ruin our play if we don't. I thought he might leave after he found out the sheriff was dead, but he shows no sign of leaving."

"Too bad the men you sent out on the road missed him," Hocker said. "You should've let me go like I wanted."

"Yeah, yeah. Should've, should've."

"Tay Redwing brought in another gun he says is top-notch. Name of John Henry Lockhart."

"Lockhart!" Polk yelled. "I know about that lunatic. He's crazier than a tree frog living in a fishpond."

"He may be, but he showed up yesterday."

Polk knew Anse Hocker well, and trusted the short, slope-shouldered man up to a point. The point at which he didn't trust Hocker was with his drinking. Hocker was a drunk. But since he held his whiskey well, he had tolerated it through the years.

The two of them, along with over three hundred other guer-

103

rilla fighters, had ridden into Lawrence, Kansas, together on August twenty-first, 1863, behind Colonel William Quantrill. They had ridden together, and had fought side by side for months alongside men who would become infamous in the years to come: men like the Youngers and the James brothers. In Lawrence, he had been witness to violence he could never have dreamed possible. Those were not combatants they were killing; those were fathers, mothers, and children. He watched as men were pulled from their homes and businesses and brought to the center of the town where they were executed, often right in front of their families. The raid on Lawrence was brutal.

"All I know about Lockhart is what Redwing told me," Hocker said. "He said Lockhart had fought with the Rebels along the border states until he decided further fighting was useless. Then one night he just packed his gear, stole a colonel's horse, and rode off into the night. Redwing said that he was tough and fast with a gun. He also said he's unpredictable. All I know for sure is that he's as big as a horse barn."

"Where is he now?"

"Holed up with Redwing. I told them to go out to the Holliday Ranch tomorrow at daybreak and keep an eye on the ranch, since we're about ready to make our move. We don't need any surprises."

"You told them to stay out of sight, didn't you? We don't want the Hollidays to start getting suspicious. That asshole, Wes Sanger, went off half-cocked and shot the old man in the leg, which could have ruined everything. We can't let that happen again. And we can't bother the Holliday girl either. She's hands off."

"I told them as much."

"The one thing we have to do is get rid of Ramsay. Even if we have to ambush him."

Hocker shook his head. "Nope, I don't think bushwhacking

an old Ranger, who's now an Underwood man, would be a good idea, Jake. That would bring every lawman in Texas down on us in a hurry. There's got to be another way."

"I don't care how you do it, just do it. Ramsay has to go."

CHAPTER TWENTY-SEVEN

Calico woke up restless. She had spent the night trying without much success to rid her mind of the unpleasant memories that came rushing back at her for some inexplicable reason. Her mind had swirled with visions of her dead parents lying in front of their burning cabin, of the greasy, strange-talking bandits who had grabbed her and tossed her into the back of a stinking wagon. Of the canyon where the Indians attacked. Of Elizano's kindness. Then there was Wolf Eye, and, of course, the corporal she had clung to for two days as they rode to the ranch. She remembered how she had cried when the troopers left her and rode away.

Why are all these memories returning? Why?

She remembered Momma Sarah's kindness, her patience, and all the sleepless nights she had spent cuddling the little lost girl, trying to make things better for her. Then she remembered the loss of Momma Sarah, and how deeply the hurt bit into her very soul.

Thoughts of Clint Ramsay would all of a sudden creep into her mind. Her feelings were in turmoil. She had Gimpy saddle her horse an hour after the morning meal and brought to the front of the main house.

"Gimpy," she said. "Remind Dad that I'm spending the night in San Reale with Maria. Miss Beatrice is fitting me for some new clothes. I'll be back late tomorrow afternoon."

"You know your father's feelings about you going out alone,"

Gimpy said. "You'd better let me ride along with you."

"I'll be fine. Just tell Dad what I said." She tapped Dusty with her leather quirt. "Let's go, Dusty."

She left the house well after the ranch hands had scattered to their jobs and her father had retreated to his work desk. The tall, dark, green-eyed detective continued to materialize in her thoughts as she rode. She wasn't sure why she was bothered by his arrival. She'd never been one to give a man a second look. Somehow this time was different—different from how she had felt about the other suitors who flocked to the ranch with flimsy excuses just to see her.

There was something about him she couldn't grasp. Something just out of reach.

She guided Dusty to her private thinking place. This had to be thought out through and through. She hadn't wanted to burden her father with her storybook problems. He had his own worries. Their foreman, Joe Peterson, had sent more hands onto the range as a precaution against anything untoward happening. They had reported back that they'd seen a few tracks here and there, but nothing seemed to be missing.

Still, she was certain something was up; she just didn't know what to make of it. Sheriff Wilhoit had been killed, Dad had been shot from ambush, and then the two Underwood detectives had shown up out of the blue. What else had happened she might not know about? She realized this country produced a special brand of tough men. She was raised around men who had to fight to preserve their holdings and their way of life. She also knew how others would come along at the least sign of weakness and take everything from them. She, of all people, knew that well; she had experienced both sides of that life.

Calico felt a shiver run along her spine as she thought about the unknown.

She stopped atop the crest of a small hill that overlooked the wild and distant landscape. She had veered off the main road to ride through the rugged country to her favorite spot as she so often did. The afternoon heat bounced off the rocks, but the view was breathtaking, yet frightening in its untamed naturalness. The rocky knob where she sat on Dusty was surrounded with ragged gullies, bramble bushes, and brush thickets. She would rest Dusty for a few moments, then head for San Reale.

She curled a strand of her hair on a finger as her mind raced with random thoughts. She regretted that she had shot at the Ranger, but he hadn't seemed upset about it. Even while he talked with her father, she kept noticing him glance in her direction, but she wouldn't let on that she saw him.

She dismounted and stood beside Dusty. The dark-brown steel dust glistened in the afternoon sun. He lowered his head and rubbed it against her shoulder. She laughed and returned the affectionate gesture by brushing her fingers through his thick, soft mane. She was absorbed by her surroundings and thoughts.

But it was time to be heading to town. Miss Beatrice would be looking for her.

CHAPTER TWENTY-EIGHT

Clint and Harley were crisscrossing through the grove of trees to the side of what was once Pinhead's cabin. They were searching for the tracks of the man who had met Marva at the cabin— and had killed her.

"He had to vamoose from this side of the cabin," Clint said. "Otherwise we would've seen him."

Harley pointed to a set of tracks that led deeper into the trees. "These might be what we're looking fer," he said. "Onliest ones that 'pear to be anyways fresh."

"Let's see where they lead."

The tracks were easy enough to follow as they wove through the trees and gullies and came out onto the stage road into San Reale. There the tracks vanished into the throng of tracks left by stagecoaches, wagons, and the horses of dozens of riders entering and leaving the town.

"Well, so much for that," Clint said. "It was worth a try."

"I'll know it if I see it agin'," Harley said. "It'll show up agin' somewhere."

"Since we're out here, let's roam around a little and see what the country looks like. Might come in handy someday."

Harley tossed a chaw of tobacco on the ground, and said, "Might at that."

CHAPTER TWENTY-NINE

Tay Redwing sat on a ridge hidden in a grove of cottonwoods. Alongside him sat John Henry Lockhart. Theirs was a mismatch of size, to be sure. John Henry stood six feet seven inches tall, and weighed north of three hundred pounds if he weighed an ounce. But Redwing knew he was as hard as a limestone rock. Redwing, who was close to a foot shorter than John Henry, had hooked up with the big man a year and a half ago after the two had met in the Nation. Both were hiding from the law. They had gone their separate ways after a while: John Henry going north, and Redwing going south where he joined up with another old running mate, Anse Hocker.

Redwing was the result of the union of a Caddo squaw and a wandering cowboy. He had been raised by his mother within her tribe and had been tolerated by her people, but never accepted by them. He had a stout, muscular build with broad, square shoulders. He stood five feet eight inches tall. The first things one noticed about Redwing were his thick arms and large hands. His round face was expressionless. This had often been mistaken by others as a sign of mental weakness. But he soon became known as the best tracker in west Texas.

Redwing left his mother's people at an early age and became a fixture along the outlaw trail. He had started on his life of crime like many before him. He stole a cow or two when he was without food, then, when he'd seen how easy it had been to outwit the white ranchers, he began to take more and more of their stock. His luck took a sudden downward turn when he found himself cornered running a stolen herd along the Texas and New Mexico border. The hired enforcers of the Cattlemen's Association had caught up with him. He had to shoot his way out, and left two men lying in his wake, one of them dead. From then on, he was destined to be on the run.

When Hocker told him he needed another good gun hand for a job they were planning, Redwing suggested Lockhart. Now he wasn't so sure that was a smart idea. They had been apart for a year and a half, and now John Henry appeared to be even more unstable than Redwing remembered.

They sat well back of the ridge, keeping a watch on the Holliday ranch house as they were told to do by Hocker. Redwing kept watch with a pair of army-issued field glasses. He didn't know what he was looking for, just that Hocker said to watch the ranch and make sure everything looked to be normal. Report back any activity that looked suspicious, or was out of the ordinary for a working ranch.

John Henry was complaining, as usual, as he pulled a bottle from his saddlebag and took a swig. They'd arrived at the ranch soon after daybreak and watched as the ranch hands scattered to their work. Redwing saw nothing but a ranch operating as expected.

Then a few minutes later, a tall, fair-haired woman walked out of the back of the ranch house where a man met her with a saddled horse. The man and woman stood there talking for a few minutes.

"Well, now," John Henry said. "What do we have here?"

Redwing saw her too, but said nothing. He knew what their orders were: watch the ranch house, take notice of any strangers coming and going, and above all, make sure nothing happened to the girl who lived there. He saw John Henry lick his lips, then take another big swig of whiskey.

The girl swung up into the saddle and rode away from the ranch. Redwing saw the look on John Henry's face.

"Leave her alone, John Henry. Anse and Jake wouldn't like it if anything happened to her. Take it from me, you don't want to get Jake on your back. Or Hocker either."

John Henry jerked his head around. "Don't you be telling me what to do, Redwing. I know my own mind. If I wanna meet up with a pretty little gal, that's what I'll do." He took another swig of the whiskey and gave out with a crude laugh. "I think I'll ride out and meet her. You can come along to keep me company. That ranch ain't going nowhere."

CHAPTER THIRTY

Calico was riding easy in the saddle on the road to San Reale. Her mind was still trying to get a handle on the thoughts swirling around in her brain. She was still miles from San Reale when she spotted two horsemen riding on an old trail that ran parallel to the stage road. She pulled Dusty to the side of the road into a patch of scrub brush, but it was too late; the men had seen her. They whipped their mounts into a run and spread out in order to cut off her avenues of escape.

"Come on, Dusty." She snapped her quirt at his flanks and rode away from the men at a dead run. But she knew it was a wasted gesture. Dusty, with his speed, held the advantage for a few minutes, but the man on the left was in position to cut her off, and the man on the right had her blocked in that direction. She reached back to her scabbard for her rifle but it wasn't there.

"Dang it," she said. Then she remembered her dad had taken it from her and had told Gimpy to hide it. She pushed Dusty for a few more minutes but knew she couldn't escape. She heard a loud coarse laugh coming from the big man on the right as she slowed. There was no place for her to go, so she pulled Dusty to a stop.

She took in a deep breath as the big man approached her. He was more than big: he was enormous. He was as tall as an oak tree, and had to weigh more than her and Dusty combined. In the midst of all this, her thoughts were on his horse. How could a horse carry such a man? The other rider was a broad-chested, dark-skinned man who wore a greasy wool shirt and dirty trousers. A battered black hat with an eagle feather dangling down at the back covered his head.

"Lookee here," the big man said, as he tossed his smoke to the ground. "A purty little gal has invited herself to a party."

"I advise you to leave me out of your party," she said. "People out here don't take kindly to men harming a woman."

"Who said anything about harming you? All I said was that we was going to have us a party, and you're invited as the special guest."

Calico turned her head away to keep the overpowering odor of sweat, mixed with the smell of whiskey and horseflesh from her nostrils. She knew most of the cowhands in the area, but these two she had never seen before.

The big man climbed off his horse and grabbed Dusty's reins in his ham-like hands. The horse jerked and lurched backwards at his rough handling. The other man sat motionless and watched in silence.

"Missy," the big one said. "Me and you need to get a little better acquainted."

"I'll bet that horse is relieved that you're on the ground," she said. "Carrying around a load of lard like you would spavin an elephant."

"Well, little girl, you're going to see what it feels like to carry a load of lard."

Calico was ready for him and had removed her foot from the stirrup. When he reached for her, she let loose with a kick that caught him under the chin.

He fell backward, but recovered with his coarse laugh. "A real spitfire, ain't you."

Calico crossed her arms in front of her and hugged herself as a sudden chill enveloped her. He came toward her again. Before she could deliver another kick, she felt him wrap one of his oversized paws around her upper arm. He was fast for a big man—and surprisingly nimble. A second later, she saw the ground rising to meet her. He had just yanked her off her horse, but her brain, slow to register what was happening, was struggling to keep pace. She hit the ground hard but continued to fight. Even with his hand still clamped around her arm, she managed to kick him in the chest, and take a bite out of his right arm.

"Dammit," he said. He backhanded her with his left hand. She fell, dazed, in a pile at his feet. He unbuckled his gun belt and let it fall to the ground.

"Redwing, you can sit back and watch if you have a mind to. I aim to have a party with this purty little gal."

Chapter Thirty-One

"Can I watch too, John Henry?"

Clint rode out of the thick brush up to the big man with his right hand positioned near his gun, all the while watching the man called Redwing.

Lockhart jerked his head around at the sound. He hesitated for a moment, stared hard at the rider, then said, "Well, fancy this. If it ain't Clint Ramsay in the flesh."

Clint looked down at Calico, who lay in the dust dazed, but alert. "Calico, you get back on your horse and get out of here right now."

She put a hand to the red, puffy welt beginning to form under her left eye, and managed to get to her feet. As she stood, she was slow to move toward her horse.

"Calico, I told you to ride, now go," Clint said, a little louder than he intended. She jumped on her horse and rode hard for several yards then, out of the corner of his eye, he saw her stop behind a thick bush.

That stubborn . . .

Lockhart took a step toward Clint and said, "You ain't got nothing on me, Ramsay. So you just move on and let me be."

"Your friend over there is looking kind of itchy-fingered. You'd better tell him to relax."

John Henry turned to Redwing. "Do as you please, Redwing. But you best be quick if you decide to slap leather with this gent. Ol' Ramsay here can shuck a gun with the best of 'em."

Clint kept his eye on Redwing as the man obviously considered the odds. Redwing returned Clint's icy stare through menacing coal-black eyes, but never moved a muscle.

"Are you the one who's been doing the bushwhacking around here, John Henry?" Clint asked. "We have a dead sheriff and a wounded rancher. Both shot from ambush. That's about your style."

"I ain't never shot nobody in Texas, ever. That's a fact. Like I said, you ain't got nothing on me."

"How about your friend over there?"

"I don't talk for him."

Clint rode over toward Redwing. "You do any shooting from behind trees, Redwing?"

"When I kill, I kill face-to-face."

Clint grinned and turned back to John Henry. "Now this is the way it is, John Henry. You can either put on that gun belt and we can settle this here and now, or you can get on that horse and ride out of the country. It's your choice."

John Henry looked around, wiping his mouth with the back of his hand.

As if reading the big man's mind, Clint said, "Harley, you can come out now. I don't think these fellows are in any mood to fight."

Harley eased Jerusalem up and out of a ravine that was obscured by the scrub brush, a Winchester in his hands.

Redwing spun around toward the ravine, then looked down at the Winchester which was pointed at him.

Harley smiled at Redwing and shot a stream of tobacco juice at the dark man's horse's hoofs. "This is your lucky day, friend. I wuz hoping you might insert yourself into this squabble."

John Henry glared at Clint. "I always wondered if I could beat you with a gun, Ramsay. But I damned well know I can beat you with my fists." He grabbed his gun belt and slung it over his saddle. "Maybe we'll meet again on my terms one day. I'll take a mighty pleasure in busting your head."

"Well now, I'm not so sure of that." Clint unbuckled his gun belt and handed it over to Harley, who still had his rifle pointed at Redwing. "Take good care of these. I'll want them back in about three minutes. Keep your eyes on Redwing while I teach John Henry some manners."

"You're going to fight me with your hands? No guns?" John Henry let out a laugh again. "There ain't nobody ever whupped me with his hands."

Clint walked up to the massive mountain of a man to let the giant have the first swing. Lockhart was quick to oblige with a big looping right-hand roundhouse that Clint sidestepped. As he did, he knocked Lockhart's arm down with a right-handed chop, and followed it with a sharp punch to the jaw with his left. Lockhart straightened up and shook his head.

Lockhart charged forward, head down into Clint's stomach, throwing both his arms around his body and lifting him off the ground. Clint groaned as John Henry crushed his midsection. In desperation, he threw back his head and smacked it into Lockhart's chin. John Henry released his grip and fell backwards. He regained his balance and once again charged at Clint. He threw a wild punch that connected in Clint's stomach, bending him over. He followed with a smashing left to Clint's jaw which brought a trickle of blood to the corner of his mouth. The giant grabbed him around the body again and squeezed. Clint managed to free his right arm and began punching Lockhart in the kidney, again and again. He punched and punched until the big man released him with a loud groan.

Clint fell to ground as John Henry backed away a step to catch his breath. One thing became clear to Clint as he lay on the ground. This was a ferocious man he had challenged. But he could see that John Henry's breathing was getting shallower and shallower.

Clint rose to his feet and went in low. He threw punch after punch at him: rib cage, stomach, then ribs again. Each punch bent the big man over a little more. Clint knew he now had the advantage. He feinted with a left, then he threw a hard right at John Henry's jaw. Then another left, then another right. John Henry went down in a pile, struggling to breathe.

Clint stood over him wide-legged, rocking back and forth. He then kicked Lockhart in the side. "Get up, John Henry. Now hear this. You, too, Redwing. If I hear of either one of you bothering that lady from this day forward, you'll answer to me. Understand?"

Clint took his gun belt from Harley and buckled it around his waist. "And if I see either of you around here again, I'm going be thinking you're part of the shooting that's going on. My advice is for you to ride on out of here while you can."

John Henry struggled to his horse and hung onto the saddle for a few seconds. He was laboring hard to get a breath. When he managed to crawl aboard, he rode away without looking back. Redwing hesitated for a moment and stared at Clint, then wheeled his horse around and left at a gallop.

"I'm afraid we ain't seen the last of them," Harley said.

Clint nodded. "Could be you're right."

Clint staggered over to a grassy spot and dropped to the ground. He put a hand to his ribs where John Henry had tried to crush him. He didn't think John Henry had broken any of his ribs, but he knew he would feel the effects of this fight for several days to come.

Calico rode out from her hiding spot, jumped off the horse, and ran over to him. She yanked off her bandanna and wiped the blood from his face. "You shouldn't have fought him with your fists. You should've had better sense than that, big as he was."

Her tanned face was flushed with excitement, but she was something to behold. He shook his head to clear his mind. "He was big, that's for sure. And he had a hard punch when it connected. But I'd guess he had gotten by over the years with a bluff based on his size. People probably took one look at him and let him have his way without argument."

"But you didn't. And that wasn't very smart of you."

"He's just pigheaded, ma'am," Harley Fry said.

Clint rolled over on his side to ease the pain a little. Calico poured water from her canteen and cleaned his face about as well as she could, then backed away a step. He was still breathing hard, and winced a time or two when he moved his body to a certain position.

"I forgot to say thank you. Both of you," she said. She then pointed a finger at Clint and added, "But you know it was all your fault, don't you?"

"My fault? How . . . ?"

"If you hadn't come sneaking around our ranch, I wouldn't have shot at you, and Dad wouldn't have taken my rifle away. If I had my rifle with me, those two men wouldn't have come within three hundred yards of me. So it was all your fault."

Clint looked over at Harley and shook his head in amazement at her logic.

"Harley, meet Calico Holliday. She took exception to me riding into their ranch. And it appears she holds on to a grudge for quite a spell. Calico, this is Harley Fry, mountain man, soldier, Ranger, and friend."

Harley made a slight bow as he got a close-up look at the young woman. "Glad to make your acquaintance, ma'am." He turned and walked over to his horse and shoved his Winchester into his scabbard.

Clint got to his feet, staggered a bit, then climbed aboard his horse. He repositioned himself in the saddle several times until he was comfortable. "Come on, Calico, we'll ride with you back to your ranch. We wouldn't want anything else to happen to you." He smiled at her and added, "I've already caused one fracas today, I don't want another one."

"No, no," she said. "Those men are long gone. I'll be safe enough now. Besides, I'm going into town to stay with a friend." She walked to her horse and rode away in a cloud of dust.

Clint watched her ride with a smile on his face, then turned to Harley. "Why don't you track those two men for a spell and see where they're headed. I'm sure John Henry didn't come to San Reale on a whim. Someone sent for him, and I'd like to know who's behind this. I'm going to follow Calico back to town at a distance just as a precaution."

"At a distance, huh?" Harley said.

Chapter Thirty-Two

Back on the streets of San Reale, Ernest Teal and his son, Willie, rode down Main Street with grim looks on their faces. Both were armed. Ernest glanced at the Cattlemen's Bank as he passed it. He couldn't see Myron Welborn, which was fine with him. The less he saw of the banker, the better.

"I hear Ramsay is staying at Martha Ann's," Ernest said. The elder Teal looked like an older version of his son, except that he was shorter by an inch, and a bit heavier around the middle. His friends, of whom he had but a few, called him Ernie. The two horsemen stopped in front of the boardinghouse and tied off their mounts. They entered the building and walked up to the desk where Martha Ann was standing.

"Does Clint Ramsay have a room here, Martha Ann?" Ernie asked.

Martha Ann put her hands on her hips and gave Ernest Teal a hard look. "Maybe he does, maybe he doesn't. Why do you need to know, Ernest?"

"If he does, and if he happens to be around, tell him that Ernie Teal wants to see him over at the Half-Moon. Me and Willie here will be there waiting for him. Tell him that."

With the message passed, Ernest Teal and his son walked out of the boardinghouse.

Martha Ann put a hand to her mouth then began wringing both her hands in her apron. "Sakes alive," she said in a low, trembling voice. "Sakes alive." She was unsure what to do. If she failed to give Ramsay the message, then the Teals could sneak up on him in an alley somewhere and shoot him. If she did pass the message, she could be party to a gunfight. She sat down, distraught that Ernest Teal had put her in this position.

What am I supposed to do?

She was still wringing her hands when Clint entered the lobby an hour later. She was standing there, staring off into space, almost in a trance. When she saw him, she walked around the desk and faced him.

"Mister Ramsay, I need to talk to you." She stood erect, her hands clasped in front of her. She knew she was on the verge of tears, but fought them back with all the willpower she could muster.

"Sure, Martha Ann, would you like to join me for a cup of coffee in the dining room? I'm hot, tired, all alone, and my ribs ache. I would take pleasure in your company."

"No . . . no, Mister Ramsay. I . . . I . . . was asked to give you a message. I didn't know what to do."

"That's okay, Martha Ann, let's have it. It can't be all that bad."

"Oh, yes it is. Two men came in a while ago and said they wanted you to come over to the Half-Moon Saloon. They said they'd be waiting for you there."

"Who were these men? What did they want to see me about?"

"Ernest Teal and his son, Willie. Willie is the cowboy you had that run-in with over at the Half-Moon. Ernest—he's the father—said to tell you they'll be waiting for you. Oh, please don't go. I'll go over there and tell them I couldn't find you."

She was near tears as Clint put an arm around her shoulder and ushered her through the doorway to the dining room.

"Don't blame yourself, Martha Ann. Sooner or later they would've found me. So don't you go worrying yourself about it, okay?"

Clint left her in the dining room, but could hear her sniffling as he walked back to the lobby. He took a deep breath, checked the loads in his Colt, and then walked out the door. The walk was slow by design, with Clint trying to think of a way out of this confrontation without a shooting. No solution came to mind.

He stopped at the doors of the Half-Moon and looked into the room. He spotted the young cowboy and another man seated at a table near the back of the room. His nerves were on edge, and he had to walk a little bent over to keep his breathing normal. His ribs ached like sin. This was no time for another fight—guns, or otherwise.

He kept his eyes on the table where the two men sat as he shuffled through the saloon. Both men watched him as he approached their table.

To Clint's surprise, both of them placed their hands flat on the table, palms down. They didn't want any trouble. He relaxed a bit, but was still wary as he walked up to the table and faced them.

"Martha Ann said you wanted to see me. Here I am."

It was the older man who spoke. That he was the cowboy's father was obvious to Clint. If not for the many years difference in their ages, they could've been mistaken for brothers.

"Ramsay, my name is Ernest Teal," he said. "I think you know my son, Willie."

Clint nodded. "We've met."

The elder Teal fidgeted with his beer glass and wouldn't look Clint in the eyes as he talked. "Look, I know I ain't been much of a father to Willie here, but just the same, you done us a good turn by not shooting him down like he deserved. I heard the talk. Nobody would've blamed you if you had, but you didn't. Now, we want to do you a good turn."

He looked at Willie. "Tell him, Willie."

Willie looked down at his hands as he spoke. "The banker said he wanted me to kill you. He said he didn't care how it was done, just as long as I did it quick. And if I did, he would tear up the mortgage on our ranch."

Clint pulled out a chair and sat down. *The banker wants me killed. Why?*

"Just who is this banker, and why would he want me killed?"

The Teals looked at each other. "Then . . . then you're not here because of the banker, Welborn?" Ernest asked.

"I don't know anyone by the name of Welborn. Furthermore, this is the first time I've ever heard his name mentioned."

Ernest gave Clint a rundown on Myron Welborn, the banker. He finished by saying, "He's quick to hand out money if you sign away everything you own, then even quicker to take it all away from you. I could name you a dozen families who've been run out of their homes by this man. But poor people like us don't have no other choice."

"It sounds like our banker friend might be scared of something," Clint said. "I think I'll go have a talk with him. It could prove to be enlightening."

Willie put up his hand. "Uh, before you go, Mister Ramsay, I'd like for you to know that I learned a hard lesson the other night in the saloon. I've been acting like a real horse's ass for a long while, and you scared the hell outta me. By all rights I should be buried up on the hill for my dumbness. I just want you to know . . . well . . . that I'm gonna try to do different from here on out."

Clint smiled at the young man. He could tell right off that it was hard for Willie to face him and make that admission. He could also tell there was more to his statement than mere words. There was a sincerity to them; a sincerity that Clint knew would stand tall for the young man in the years to come.

"You might make a real man yet, Willie."

He reached over and shook the Teals' hands, then marched out of the saloon and toward the Cattlemen's Bank.

CHAPTER THIRTY-THREE

Clint gave considerable thought to how he would go about handling the information the Teals passed along to him about the banker. It seemed to him that the banker must be guilty of something in his past that he didn't want to come to light. Whatever it was, it was serious enough that the banker was willing to risk a killing to keep it hidden. Clint decided the best way to approach Welborn was to be the man Welborn thought he was—someone out to get him.

When he entered the bank, Clint marched straight toward Welborn's office. The bank teller watched him with little interest. The office door, with Myron Welborn's name and position—president—painted on it in gold letters, was closed. Clint could hear muted voices behind the door. He flipped the latch and walked in. The man he presumed to be Welborn was standing behind a desk with a woman Clint hadn't seen before; they were talking in low voices. He walked over, grabbed Welborn by the scruff of the neck, and flung him into his chair. He then took the woman by the arm and pushed her into another chair near the window.

"What's the meaning . . . Ramsay! What . . . what's going . . . ?" Welborn was blubbering and whimpering. He threw an arm across his face as if to hide from this man's intrusion into his sacred realm.

"Shut up," Clint said. "I have some business to transact with you. I'm a detective with the Underwood Agency out of Kansas

City. We have a few things to discuss, I think."

He turned to the woman, who had her hand to her mouth. "You can leave if you so desire. This business is between me and the banker."

Siena Welborn started to get out of the chair, then abruptly sat back down. A rebellious look appeared on her face as she said, "No. If it involves my husband, I want to hear it."

"Suit yourself," Clint said. "Just sit there and keep your mouth shut."

He turned to Welborn. "Our agency has been contracted by a man concerning some old business that needs straightening out."

"I . . . I don't know what you're talking about. Get out of my office."

"Sure, you know. So, here's the deal. This man hired me to do one of two things. He's giving you a choice. A better choice than you gave him, I might add. In fact, I tried to talk him out of it, but he said no. He insisted that I give you a choice, so here it is. Choice one is that I just shoot you outright. A single bullet in the head. Messy, but effective. He suggested it be right between your eyes so you can see it coming. Choice two is that you tell the sheriff why the man who hired me wants revenge, and what brought it on. With choice one, you die quick, with choice two, you live."

"Myron, don't listen to him," Siena shouted. "He won't shoot you. He won't do it. Don't say a word. He's bluffing."

"Time's wasting, banker," Clint said. He spun the cylinder on his Colt and put the cold steel on Myron's forehead. "I don't give a damn which option you choose. This is just a job with me. I get paid the same either way. I was just obliged to make the offer. So which is it banker, a bullet in the head, or life?"

"Don't say a word," Siena cried. "He won't shoot you."

Welborn was sobbing now, ignoring Siena's pleas. She continued to shout at him to shut up.

"Okay, no choice is the same as choice number one, banker." Clint thumbed back the hammer on his gun. "Tell your pretty little wife good-bye. And you'd better tell her where you have all your cash hidden. It looks like she's accustomed to the good life."

"No, wait, wait," Welborn shrieked. "Maybe I did make a mistake or two in the past, but . . ."

"Names, banker. I want names." Clint pressed the gun to Welborn's head harder. "Time's running out. Do we go tell Elder names, or do I pull the trigger?"

"Trimble, Abel Trimble," Welborn shouted.

"You old fool," Siena said. "Now see what you've done? You'll be the one in prison now."

"Go on, banker. Tell the rest now that you've started."

Welborn wiped at his eyes, reached up and pushed Clint's gun aside. "I forged his mortgage papers and took his ranch." He then looked up at Clint with pleading eyes and said, "But he got his revenge. He shot up my bank, and it cost me four thousand dollars to repair the damage."

Clint backed away a step and pointed his gun toward the door. "Let's go."

"Look, Ramsay, let's make a deal," Welborn said. "I can pay you more than Trimble can pay you. Just forget all about this and I'll pay you two, no, I'll pay you three times what Trimble promised you, and nobody will ever know."

"Not enough. I have a reputation to protect. Now we're going to march over to the sheriff's office and tell Sam Elder all about this Trimble deal. Get on your feet."

But Welborn wasn't giving up quite so easily. Clint knew the banker's mind was racing to find a way out of this tight spot. And he wasn't wrong.

"Look," Welborn said, standing alongside Ramsay. "What if I tell you who killed Ed Wilhoit? Will that satisfy you?"

Clint's muscles tensed. "You know who shot Ed? Who is this man? Tell me now."

Siena jumped up and grabbed Myron by the throat. "No Myron, don't say another word. Not another word."

Clint pulled her off the banker and shoved her to the floor. He pointed the gun at Myron's forehead again. "Who is the man and where can I find him? Tell me this minute if you want to live."

"Do we have a deal? I'll tell you if we have a deal."

"My deal is to start shooting you if you don't tell me. I'll start with the legs and work up to your head. It'll be slow and painful, I assure you. Now, start talking."

Welborn wiped at his eyes and looked at Siena. "I don't have any choice. I have to tell him."

At the same time Welborn was making that statement, Clint caught a glimpse of movement at the window—a gun. He grabbed Welborn around the waist and tried to drop the two of them to the floor. A shot and the sound of shattering glass reverberated in the small office as they both fell. Ramsay still had Welborn clutched around the waist as they hit the floor. He lay still, waiting for another shot, but none came. He raised his head and pushed the banker's body off him. He looked at Welborn and saw blood foaming around his mouth, and blood on his suit coat. Welborn had taken the bullet that was meant for Clint. He was dead, no question. Siena sat huddled in the far corner of the office, pale and shaking.

The shot had come through the side window of his office. Clint rushed to the window and caught a glimpse of a man rounding the corner of the bank building. He fired, but the man disappeared before he could get off a second round. He looked at Welborn again, but it was clear that the banker was dead. He was considering what to do next when Siena decided for him.

She began screaming, "You've killed him. You've killed Myron. Help, help! Somebody get the sheriff. Ramsay has killed Myron."

Clint knew he was in trouble. This woman was cool under pressure and was quick to see how to twist this incident against him. He had at best a few minutes to act. If he stayed, he'd either be locked up by Sam Elder, innocent or not, or he'd have to shoot his way out. He wanted neither. He looked around and spotted a rear office door that led to an alley. He holstered his gun and ran toward the door.

He looked back at Siena and said, "You're getting off lucky this time, lady. But we'll be seeing each other again, you can count on it."

He hurried through the rear office doorway, stopped at the corner of the building, and looked in all directions. He didn't know the backstreets and alleyways of San Reale, but he was confident that the livery stable was a few blocks to the east of where he stood. He inched himself in that direction, careful not to be seen or heard. He suspected that Sam Elder was already on his way to the bank and would be forming a search party for him within minutes. His best hope was to get to the stable and Buck ahead of them. As he approached the stable, he could hear loud voices coming from where he thought the stable was located.

Too late.

He leaned his back against the rough siding of a building and tried to figure out his next move. Without a horse, he was sure to be found sooner or later. San Reale wasn't large enough of a town in which to disappear for any length of time. The voices were beginning to get louder and closer. He heard a gunshot in the distance.

Someone shooting at shadows.

He was running out of time and options. Then he heard footsteps behind him. He turned, went down on one knee, and drew his gun at the same time. Someone was approaching, taking quick strides. He hugged the wall of the building, pointed his pistol at the sound of the footsteps, and waited for the person to show.

Chapter Thirty-Four

"Don't shoot, don't shoot."

As the person got closer, he could see that it was Calico Holliday.

"Quick," she said. "I've got two horses over in the trees. The folks out there aren't in much of a listening mood right now, so we have to hurry. I don't know what went on in that bank, but Sam Elder has them searching for you everywhere in town. We don't have time to waste, unless you prefer to be the honored guest at a hanging party."

Clint grabbed Calico by the shoulders. "Thanks for the horse, but you stay here. You can't get involved with this. This is my problem, not yours."

"Quit arguing and ride. I know this country better than anyone else. Now let's go."

She hadn't yet finished her sentence when Clint felt splinters of wood hit his face as a bullet crashed into the wall next to him. She was right; this was no time to be arguing. He ducked low and ran toward the trees where a ragged-looking mustang stood next to Dusty. More shots were fired as he climbed into the worn saddle and left San Reale at a gallop, a few yards behind Calico.

She ran Dusty all out for several miles, then cut hard left into a brush-covered ravine where the two of them traveled for another half mile. She then climbed out of the long, narrow ravine onto a grass-covered animal trail. She held up her hand

and slowed Dusty to a walk.

"We're safe for the time being," she said. "Elder and his posse won't find our trail."

"You shouldn't be doing this. There's still time for you to ride away and no harm done. They don't know about you helping me get away. Besides, you're getting yourself tangled up with a murder. I don't think your father would appreciate you helping a murderer escape the law."

"Dad will understand when I explain. I was walking by the bank door when I heard all the commotion going on inside. I stopped to see what was happening when I heard the shot. Then I saw a man running in the alley and another shot. Right after that I heard a woman screaming that you had shot Welborn. I had a pretty good idea it wasn't you who shot Welborn. Was I right?"

"That's the way it happened. I didn't see who shot the banker, but it wasn't me. I'm sure I was the target, but the banker got in the way of the bullet. That still doesn't mean you have to get involved. There's time for you to ride away."

She grinned. "Well . . . maybe not. There's a couple of things you ought to know. Somebody in San Reale is going to be pretty mad when he finds his mustang missing. That makes me an accomplice to whatever it was you did, and worse, it makes me a horse thief, big as life."

He gave her an admiring look. Here she was: tall, graceful, beautiful, stubborn, independent, and not afraid to do what had to be done, the devil take the consequences.

"Okay, Calico. It looks like you're stuck with me whether we like it or not."

He glanced over his shoulder at their back trail. His first thought was to find a place to provide the two of them adequate cover for the night: a place to give him time to think, time to plan. He rode up beside her.

"First we have to elude Elder and his posse for a day or two while they've got lynching on their mind. Our explanations can come later when cooler heads prevail. So, where can we go?"

Calico pointed to the low broken hills that were stretched out in front of them. "I know of a place about midway up in those hills where we can hide until this storm blows over. It's a long ride, so we need to be on the move while we still have some daylight left."

He slapped the mustang on the flanks and followed her as she headed for the hills.

Chapter Thirty-Five

Harley Fry was wedged between two small saplings on a ridge that overlooked a homestead which appeared to have been abandoned years before. The main house was on its last legs. The wooden siding had rotted, the roof had collapsed in the middle, and weeds that surrounded the house had grown to chest high. But that was where John Henry and Redwing had led him, so he decided to get a closer look at the place.

He had left Jerusalem tied to a willow tree near a small stream a quarter of a mile behind him. There was plenty of sweet grass around the horse to keep him occupied for hours if need be. Between him and the house was a scattering of scrub brush and what was once pasture and cropland, now gone back to nature. He entertained no concern about cover as he crept up to get a closer look at the place. As he got nearer, he could see no activity around the house. Then he saw why. The place was about to fall in on itself.

Harley turned his attention to the nearby gable-roofed barn. It was a large, sturdy structure with a hay loft above the stable area. It appeared to him that the homesteaders who had once lived there thought more of their barn than they did of their house. He stretched out on his stomach in the high grass and scanned the barn through his spyglass. A crude corral had been constructed behind the barn and held several horses and mules. Two men moved out of a lean-to attached to the rear of the barn: not Redwing or John Henry. From his vantage point

Harley watched the two men, who were wearing wide sombreros and woven cloth serapes. They began forking hay to the stock inside the corral. A large black dog accompanied them.

Mexican mule skinners. With a dog.

Harley crept closer to the barn to get a better look at what was going on inside. No barking from the dog yet! Maybe his luck would hold out for another quarter hour. He circled around to the side of the barn off to his right to avoid the lean-to and the mule skinners. They had a big fire going and were roasting some kind of animal on a spit. The smoke and the smell of roasting meat drifted straight toward him. The two men threw down their pitchforks and were joined by a third man. They sat huddled together, oblivious to the world spinning around them. As he got closer, he could hear their insistent chatter.

He continued to move toward the front of the barn, careful to avoid making any noise. Since he was upwind of the barn, that reduced the likelihood that the mongrel dog might get a whiff of his scent. Plus, the smell wafting up from the roasting animal would help as well. When he reached the corner of the barn, he lowered himself to his stomach again and took a quick look around. He saw a smaller fire in front of the barn door, well off to his right. The two men he'd followed, Redwing and John Henry, sat by the fire on makeshift benches, taking turns pulling down from a whiskey bottle. They too were oblivious to the world spinning around them.

He eased himself backwards toward the low-cut portion of a Dutch door on the side of the barn. Still on his stomach, he slithered through the lower section of the door and found himself in back of two wagons, both of which were covered with canvas. He stopped for a second to listen, then peeked into the wagons one by one. He found nothing suspicious in them except for the quantity: boxes of trail supplies, barrels of water, flour, meal, dried fruit, coffee, and a few cartons of cartridges.

Somebody was preparing to go on a long trip. The smell of cured bacon in one of the wagons set his stomach to growling, so he moved on. When he turned back toward the door, he noticed in the far corner a box covered by a thick quilt. He moved over to it, lifted the edge of the quilt, and was surprised at what he saw:

Farraday Ammunitions Company
High Explosives—Handle with Care

Dynamite! He retraced his steps back out of the barn. Outside, he decided to take one more look at the two men seated around the smaller fire before he left. When he returned to the corner of the barn, he saw there were now three men sitting there. The third man seemed to be drawing something in the dust with a stick. *A map maybe?* He couldn't hear what they were saying, but the man made frequent gestures with his hands as they stared at the drawing in the dust.

He watched them for a few more minutes and then slipped away from the barn. He'd reached the scrub brush when his worst fears materialized. The mongrel dog began barking and running in his direction. He buried his face in the ground and remained as still as he could manage. He heard the mule skinners shouting and the sound of running feet.

He knew he was in trouble—big trouble.

Harley was contemplating his meager choices. He could make a dash for Jerusalem and try to outrun them, or he could stand his ground and make a fight of it. Then, to his everlasting surprise, a third choice presented itself. He heard a rifle shot from behind the barn, then another one. After the shots, the shouting subsided, but the dog kept yapping. Harley raised his head and looked toward the barn. The three mule skinners and the three men from the front of the barn were standing in a circle looking down at an antelope one of them had shot and killed. He watched from his vantage point for several more minutes. The circle then broke up and the men returned to their campfire.

The mule skinners became preoccupied with skinning the antelope while Redwing, John Henry and the other man turned their attention back to the dusty ground. While this was going on, Harley slipped back to the stand of willows, mounted Jerusalem, and left the area.

On the way back to San Reale, he gave silent thanks to an unfortunate antelope who had arrived in the nick of time.

CHAPTER THIRTY-SIX

Clint continued to follow Calico as she zigzagged along the rocky foothills, often changing directions and veering off their route to confuse the posse should they stumble upon their trail. He'd begun to see what kind of person had come to his rescue. She had learned the survival skills so necessary for living in this barren country. He was quick to see that she was an accomplished horseman—or horsewoman, in her case. Every move she made was made with ease and efficiency. No wasted motion or energy.

He soon realized they had been near the spot where she was headed all along. But she had delayed taking him there until darkness had settled in, just in case someone was observing them from afar. They had ridden the last three hours in silence, both too intent upon reaching the hills and covering their trail for conversation. But he watched her with increased admiration as she went about her task with full attentiveness to each detail.

When darkness settled in and the shadows enveloped them, she stopped and pointed toward a steep, rocky slope off to their left. "We need to dismount and lead our horses up this slope. But be careful. It's steep, and can get tricky in the dark."

Clint did as he was told. It was slow going for the horses. About halfway up the winding slope, he saw where they were headed. Calico was leading him to an almost-hidden rocky overhang, which sat back from a narrow ledge. It was partially obscured with brush and fallen boulders, but was, for all practical purposes, a cave large enough to provide shelter for several people and their stock.

In the center of the overhang, he found a blackened fire pit, and at the rear of the cave he saw a stack of dried wood left behind by a previous inhabitant. He led the horses to the back of the cave and unsaddled them. He gave them a quick rubdown, and stashed their meager gear against the rear rock wall. He then walked to the mouth of the overhang and observed their surroundings from that vantage point. There was little for him to see as night had fallen, but he knew somewhere out there was a posse searching for him.

The day's heat had dissolved into an appreciated coolness as a stiff breeze drifted through the hills. The sky above him was clear, with a three-quarter moon and millions of flickering stars watching over them. He returned to where Calico was seated on a chunk of wood near the fire pit. She had started a small fire on which she had placed a rusty coffeepot.

"I had a little jerky and a pouch of coffee in my bags," she said. "I found this rusty pot and a couple of tin cups. It will do the trick if you like a little iron in your coffee."

"Iron will taste good." He sat down across the stone fire pit from her. He was tired, both physically and mentally. His muscles still ached from his fight with John Henry, and his temples throbbed as if a Comanche warrior were beating on a war drum inside his head. Even so, he wasn't about to let Calico know how he felt. She had risked everything, including her very life, to save him from the mob forming in San Reale.

"Some place you have here," he said, as he waved his hand around the cave. "How did you find it?"

"Gimpy brought me here long, long ago. He doesn't talk much about the old days, but I think he might've been involved in some shady enterprises in his past. This is one of the places where he took refuge when things got too hot for him in civilization. Considering all the things I had experienced in my life, I think he realized that I needed a place like this to come to from time to time."

She looked into his green eyes amid the flickering of the fire then added, "But I've never told anyone else about this place. It was mine and Gimpy's secret. Until now."

"Your secret is safe with me. What about water? There seems to be everything here we need but water."

"Off to the right a few yards is a stone basin around three feet deep. It was hewn out of the rocks thousands of years ago by a trickle of water that flows into it from up above. We'll have plenty of water for us and the horses for a few days if we use a little care."

Clint straightened up and walked over to Dusty and the mustang. "I'll water the horses and fill our canteens while the coffee is boiling."

When he returned with the horses, Calico was standing at the fire, running her fingers through her long tresses. She appeared calm, relaxed, unafraid of him, and unconcerned about what lay ahead. He wondered if that was an act for his benefit, or if it came from deep within, a product of her upbringing. He regretted that she'd become involved in his troubles, but then, without her, it was likely that he'd be either dead or in jail.

He was on the verge of telling her his thoughts, when she said, "The coffee's ready, and there's a little jerky lying on that rock. Help yourself."

Then she walked away from him.

CHAPTER THIRTY-SEVEN

The third man Harley had seen at the homestead fire was Anse Hocker. He had hurried out to the homestead when he learned of the shooting at the bank. Now that Ramsay was on the run, they were presented with an opportunity to get rid of him without arousing the town with another ambush shooting.

"Redwing," he said. "I want you to track Ramsay and finish him off. Take Lockhart with you. The talk in town is that Ramsay has the Holliday girl with him. But she's not to be harmed, remember that. I want Ramsay buzzard bait, but the girl left alone, understand?"

Hocker saw a curious look pass between his two gunmen, but it soon vanished. Redwing he knew would follow orders; Lockhart, well, he didn't know. He reached into his pocket and pulled out a few coins. He flipped one of the twenty-dollar gold coins in the air. "Jake said he would give each of you a fifty-dollar bonus if you get Ramsay."

John Henry wiped his mouth and said, "We'll get him. That fifty dollars is as good as mine. You just keep it handy."

Tay Redwing and John Henry slowed their horses as they approached the outskirts of San Reale. They had left the homestead soon after Hocker had departed. Redwing figured they had an hour of daylight left, then another thirty minutes of dusk before they would have to call it quits for the night.

Outside of San Reale, it took Redwing all of three minutes to find the clear trail left by Elder's posse. He leaned over his horse's neck and gave out a loud snort. "Eight men in posse. Wipe out Ramsay trail." He pointed to the northeast. "They go that way. To the hills. Good place to hide."

The area ahead of them was ripe with gullies, eroded ravines, and thick patches of underbrush, making the going difficult. But Redwing knew that was the type of terrain a running man like Ramsay would choose. He slapped his horse on the rump, and rode wide of the posse's tracks. He was confident the posse would never find Ramsay, and would play out before sunset, then head back to San Reale. That would make finding Ramsay's tracks much easier.

Redwing also knew that John Henry was paying little attention to the trail, or anything else around them. He was already counting the extra fifty dollars that Hocker promised each of them when they got Ramsay.

"I figure it this way," John Henry said to Redwing. "With this extra fifty dollars, along with the five hundred Anse promised us when the job is done, we can live pretty high on the hog for a couple months."

"Got to catch first. And you need to hope Polk not find out about you and girl back there."

"I can handle Polk," John Henry said.

Redwing said: "Like you handle Ramsay?"

They rode as fast and hard as their horses could carry them on the broken ground which was flush with dead ends, gullies, and rocky terrain. Twice they had to turn around and find another path. But Tay Redwing never wavered in his belief that Ramsay was somewhere up ahead of them. And he never wavered in his belief that sooner or later he would cut the trail of the two riders. They'd been riding for close to an hour when he saw the shinning glint of a broken rock that lay in a narrow ravine. Then a little farther along, he saw the spot where two horses had climbed out of the ravine.

He smiled. He had found their trail. And when he found it, he knew where Ramsay and the girl were headed.

CHAPTER THIRTY-EIGHT

Clint sat and stared at the fire while he sipped the steaming coffee from the rusty cup. Calico sat across from him doing the same. There was an uncomfortable silence between them. He noticed that the night air had begun to have a bite to it, so he said, "It could get cold up here tonight. How are you fixed for a blanket?"

The mustang Calico had pilfered for him had a blanket roll and rain slicker tied to the saddle. He was prepared to hand them over to his blue-eyed guide.

"I'll make out," she said. "I have a blanket."

Clint stirred the coals under the coffeepot with a small stick. While he looked at the glowing coals, he said, "What will your father think of you running away with a wanted man? Then spending the night all alone with him in a cave?"

"He'll just have to understand, that's all. If he doesn't understand, that's too bad. I'll know the truth, and that's all that matters. If he has any issues with my motives, he'll just have to deal with them."

Clint stopped stirring the coals and looked at her. "I know I've put you in a terrible position and I regret it." He set the stick aside, and walked over to her. "I'll admit up front that I regret it with mixed feelings, since you saved my life, but at the same time this could put you in a bad light if word gets out. I'll be leaving this country in a few days, but this is your home. I wouldn't have people think ill of you for anything."

"Are you afraid to spend the night here with me?" she asked, with a twinkle in her eyes.

He shrugged his shoulders. "Could be," he said. "You're a fine-looking young lady."

"I know that Sam Elder, or his posse, doesn't scare you a whit. I've already seen you fight a tougher man than him and bring him to his knees. But you know what I think?"

He was uncertain where she was headed, so he reacted before she could speak. He took a step closer and pulled her to her feet. She faced him without flinching. He took her by the shoulders, drew her close to him and kissed her. He backed away a step, looked into her blue eyes, then leaned in and kissed her again. To his amazement, Calico threw her arms around his neck and returned his kisses with an eagerness that surprised him.

Then, just as quickly, she dropped both her arms and hurried over to the rear of the cave where she had prepared her makeshift bed.

Calico rolled herself up in a multicolored blanket with her back to Clint and the fire. She pulled the blanket up under her chin and stared at the rock wall, her mind spinning with conflicting thoughts. Here she was helping a gunman escape the law—a gunman who made her heart beat a little faster each time he looked at her. And he had kissed her. And she had wanted him to kiss her.

What was happening to her? She'd never felt these wild, startling emotions before. Why now? She stared at the rock wall as if the answer would appear. Was it gratitude she felt for his whipping John Henry and saving her on the trail, or was it something deeper? She didn't know. She had no experience from which to draw a conclusion. The one thing she did know was that this man's presence bothered her in some unfamiliar way.

Much later, she rolled over and looked in his direction in the darkness. She heard his faint snoring and heavy breathing. *There he is,* she thought, *sleeping like a baby with half the country looking for him. He has no fear. Why am I even thinking about him? I'll wake up one day next week, and he'll be gone! He as much as told me that.*

But one thing was clear to her as she lay there. Clint Ramsay was here now, and he hadn't finished what he'd started in San Reale. With that one clear thought in her mind, Calico drifted off to peaceful sleep.

On the other side of the overhang, Clint dozed on and off during the night, alert to any noises. Several times he heard small varmints as they scooted along the hard-packed floor of the cave. Far to the west, he had heard a few rumbles of thunder and had seen the distant flash of lightning. During his waking hours, he found himself reliving everything that had occurred that day. The conversation with the Teals, the death of the banker, the coolness of the banker's wife, the fortuitous appearance of Calico and the mustang—and most of all, Calico's response to his kisses.

It was ironic, he thought, that after all the years of him chasing outlaws, now it was him being chased, and for something he hadn't done. The tables had been turned, and he was on the run.

He took one last look in Calico's direction before his weariness got the best of him and he dropped off to sleep again.

CHAPTER THIRTY-NINE

Clint awoke the next morning with the sun shining in his eyes. He felt refreshed, but hungry. He stood and stretched his arms and back. As much as he liked soft mattresses, the bed he had thrown together on the rocky ground last night seemed to work just fine for his tired, aching body. He picked up his gun belt lying by his blanket and strapped it on before doing anything else. Then he looked over toward Calico's blanket. She was still wrapped up in the blanket asleep.

He made his way to the opening and peered out into the distant wasteland. The sun was up over the horizon, warming the sand, the rocks, the rattlers, and everything else that called this land home. He wished he had Harley's spyglass. But after a careful scan of the area, he could see nothing that concerned him. He returned to the fire pit and stirred the coals under the rusty coffeepot. He threw on a few more sticks of wood and added water to the pot from Calico's canteen.

Before long, he heard the rustling of a blanket in Calico's direction. He glanced over and saw her moving around. She sat up and yawned, then rubbed the sleep from her eyes.

"Good morning," he said. He was reluctant to start a conversation with her, not knowing how she might react after last night's impromptu show of affection. "I believe we've got just enough coffee left for a couple cups apiece, although they might be a little on the weak side."

She got to her feet, pulled her long blonde hair back, and

tied it behind her head with a blue ribbon. After she rolled up her blanket and secured it behind her saddle, she joined him as he stood beside the fire.

"Thanks," she said. She sipped at the coffee, not looking in his direction.

Clint did the same, bringing about another uncomfortable silence between the two of them.

After a prolonged silence, Calico said, "Clint, do we need to talk about last night?"

He looked at her and smiled. "What do you think?"

"That's not fair," she said, looking into her coffee cup. "We've known each other for what, three days?"

He took a step toward her and put his hands around her face and gazed into her eyes. "Tell you what, Calico. Let's you and me get ourselves out of this little predicament we're in, then we'll talk about it, real serious like. What do you say? It could be that I might have a lot to say to you—and it could take a while."

She pressed her hands to his. "Don't play games with me, Clint Ramsay. You know I'm a crack shot."

He bent over and gave her a soft kiss on her forehead. "No games, Calico. I promise. But let's get out of this jam first, then we'll have a long talk."

She squeezed his hands against her face and nodded. "It's a deal. Now, have you taken a look outside yet?"

"There's not a thing in sight that I could see." He took a final sip of the coffee then threw the dregs into the fire. "I'm going to lead the horses down to the water tank and take another good look around while they drink. I noticed clumps of grass growing in the rock crevices, so I'll gather a few of those while I'm at it. Horses get hungry too you know."

"I'm fresh out of jerky, so if you see a jackrabbit you might grab it."

He saddled the two horses and led them to the opening. The last thing he wanted would be for them to need to make a quick escape and have two horses left to saddle. He nudged the horses from the overhang onto the rocky ledge, keeping to as much cover as he could find.

John Henry was getting impatient. Redwing had told him not to worry about the trail as darkness had closed in on them. Using his Indian instincts, Redwing had kept them riding toward the broken hills in front of them in the dark. He told John Henry he was sure that's where Ramsay and the woman were headed. That's where he would go if he were being chased by a posse.

They had stopped just short of the hills and caught a quick two hours of sleep, then were back on the trail well before daybreak. The sun had just risen above the horizon when Redwing spotted the runaways' tracks again. The tracks of the two horses had wandered around, then all of a sudden led to a steep slope that rose to a ledge thirty feet or more above the rocky floor.

"Up there," Redwing said.

"You sure it's them?"

"Redwing sure."

Minutes later, Redwing saw Ramsay as he walked onto the ledge to look around. But his sudden appearance surprised him, and he wasn't ready to shoot. Then, before he could get his rifle positioned, Ramsay had disappeared back into the overhang.

Redwing and John Henry settled in behind a large boulder to see if Ramsay would show himself again. And he did. But he was still obscured by the brush, making a sure kill shot iffy. Redwing sat back and waited. He was going to kill Ramsay, that was for certain, and he didn't mind the wait. John Henry wanted that extra fifty dollars, but Redwing wanted the kill.

Redwing knew that Ramsay had to come down from the

rocky overhang sooner or later. When he did, he would be waiting for him with a hot reception. He was certain he'd thought of everything. As insurance, he'd instructed John Henry to be ready for a follow-up shot in case he missed. But he didn't intend to miss.

"Remember what I say," Redwing said. "I shoot first. If he not drop on my shot, you shoot. You not shoot before me, you hear?"

John Henry looked at him, but did not answer.

Redwing stepped up to him and said again, "You hear?"

"Yeah, yeah, I heard you. You shoot first. But you'd better not miss him."

Redwing eased himself back behind the boulder as far as he could, while still giving himself room to make the shot when it came. Then he saw movement again above him. Ramsay was holding a tin cup, looking out at the land before him once again.

Making sure no one is around.

"Be ready," Redwing said.

After five minutes, Redwing heard the sound of hoofs hitting rocks above them. "He comes." He saw Ramsay walk out onto the ledge leading two horses. Ramsay hesitated for a moment, then walked along the ledge, keeping the horses between him and the edge of the cliff.

"Too far back," Redwing said. "Not get shot at him."

Then Ramsay reappeared, bending over from the waist, then standing, then bending over again.

"What's he doing?" John Henry asked.

"Pulls grass for horses. Get closer to ledge."

Redwing watched as Ramsay walked along the edge of the cliff, getting closer to his range with each step. He sighted in, and then he pulled the trigger.

CHAPTER FORTY

Clint had pulled loose another clump of sweet grass when he thought he saw movement behind a boulder far below him. Or was it his imagination? He dropped the clump of grass and fell flat on the ground just in case. He reached for the butt of his holstered Colt when he hit the ground, but the gun had fallen out of his holster and lay near the ledge. That's when he felt a slash on the side of his head, and then heard the sound of a rifle, followed by another blast. He rolled over toward the water tank as far from the ledge as he could go. The mustang had begun to buck and spin around in fright, creating a dust devil that obscured everything for a moment. Soon Dusty joined the mustang in the improvised dance.

Clint breathed a sigh of relief that he had escaped with a slight wound to the head. He lay back against the edge of the crevice and waited. Was it Sam Elder and a posse? He doubted it. If it were the law, they would have shouted out at him before shooting, knowing that Calico was with him. No, it had to be the unknown bushwhackers at work again. He heard two more shots, neither hitting close enough to him to cause much concern. He looked around. There was plenty of water—but nothing else except solid rock walls in every direction. He was safe enough where he was, but if he tried to get back to the cave, he would be exposed to the shooter.

I'm trapped.

Clint then had a chilling thought as he surveyed the area in which he lay. Sure, he was safe, but what about Calico?

Then the shooting stopped. Clint was still stretched out on his stomach, waiting for some sign, a shout, hoofbeats, anything. But none came. Still, he was sure the shooter hadn't left and was just biding his time. He looked around once more. Sheer, smooth rock walls behind him, and the ledge in front. The only way out was the way he came in, and his Colt was lying ten feet away, out of his reach. There might even be more than one shooter. A second shooter could be circling around looking for a better vantage point as he lay there.

Clint waited, lying prone at the back the ledge for a full half hour or more. Still, no more shots were fired. Could he have been wrong? Maybe the shooter had left. Should he chance a look? Little by little he eased himself over to the edge of the cliff to take a look. He neither saw nor heard anything. He waited another quarter hour then looked again. Still quiet, no more shots. He decided the ambusher had left. Using extreme caution, he raised himself upon his knees. That's when he felt a bullet hit him in the side.

"Got Ramsay," Redwing said. He crouched and moved to the edge of the boulder and showed himself for a brief moment, then ducked back in. No shots from the ledge. "Dead, or hit bad. Not return fire."

"Let's go up there and finish him off if he's still breathing," John Henry said. "You take care of him. I'll take care of the girl."

Redwing glared at the big man but said nothing.

The two bushwhackers slipped out from behind the boulder and ran to the trail leading up the slope to the overhang. Redwing darted from one side of the slope to the other as he climbed toward the ledge where Ramsay lay. John Henry lumbered along a few steps behind him. As they got closer,

Redwing became more convinced than ever that he'd killed Ramsay with that last shot. The fact that he had never even once shot back at them convinced him.

"Have you seen the woman?" John Henry asked. "Are you sure she's up there with him?"

"She there. No place to hide. We get Ramsay, woman not problem."

John Henry wiped his mouth with the back of his hand.

Clint's senses had begun to return little by little. He still lay on his back staring at the blue, cloudless sky. What had happened? Then it came to him. *I've been shot.* Feeling his head, he felt the sticky ooze, but realized that the first bullet had just grazed his skull and had not caused irreparable damage. How much time had passed? Was the bushwhacker still out there, or was he approaching him as he lay there immobile? He was exhausted, his head pounding. Then he noticed blood on his shirt. He felt the hole in the shirt, then the wound. He'd taken a piece of lead in his lower side as well as the head. That was why he was so weak. He was losing blood fast. The sky began spinning above him. He shut his eyes to rest for a moment.

Just a few seconds of rest, that's all I need.

He lay on the ground too weak to move. He knew he'd lost a lot of blood. Then he heard a voice telling him to be still, to quit moving. He struggled to open his eyes, but they wouldn't cooperate. He dared not raise his head again, not knowing how many men were out there. He became aware of movement around him, but he was unable to think with a clear head, or understand what was happening.

Then someone began talking to him. *Calico!*

"Be still," she said. "I crawled out on the ledge and got your gun while those men were coming up the slope and couldn't see me. I'll not make it easy for them if they come much closer."

He felt her grab him under the arms and drag him back away from the ledge toward the water basin. Calico ripped open his shirt and tore off a piece. She rolled it up and jammed it into the jagged wound in his side. He groaned at the pain, but remained conscious.

"You're losing blood, so maybe that'll help plug up the hole."

Clint felt her warmth as she lay down beside him. And then he heard the click as she pulled back the hammer on the Colt.

"Who . . . is . . . it?"

"John Henry and that Redwing guy, the two men from the trail. I caught a glimpse of them as they started up the slope. I'm pretty sure they didn't see me. Now you be quiet and let me handle it."

"But . . ."

"Shush. I'm a better shot with my rifle," she whispered. "But I'll make 'em think twice about coming up that slope. All the military experts say to take the high ground for a battle, don't they? Well, we've got the high ground and I plan on keeping it."

The two bushwhackers were ten feet from the overhang opening when Tay Redwing stepped out from behind a rock. As he did, a bullet hit the wall a foot from his face, sending shards of sharp rock flying in all directions. He fell flat on his stomach, feeling the sting of cuts on his neck and face.

"He not dead. He trick us." Redwing was not in any position to move in any direction but back down the slope; otherwise Ramsay was sure to see him. Another bullet hit close to him, scattering more shards of rock around him. Blood began streaming down his face. He raised his hands to his face and began scratching in a futile effort to ease the stinging sensations brought on by the sharp rock fragments.

Behind him, John Henry started backtracking down the slope to their original position behind the boulder. Redwing soon followed, his face covered with bloody gashes and cuts. He took out a filthy handkerchief and began dabbing at the cuts.

"What're we going to do now?" John Henry asked. "He sure as hell ain't dead like you thought."

Redwing looked behind him and pointed toward a swirl of dust two, maybe three miles away. "Riders. Maybe posse. We go."

"What about my fifty dollars? And that purty girl?"

Redwing had already retreated to his horse and was in the saddle. "I ride."

John Henry let loose a string of cusswords, then ran to his horse and followed close behind Redwing.

CHAPTER FORTY-ONE

Calico heard the sound of running horses. She raised her head and saw the two men riding away from where she and Clint lay. A few minutes later, as she was debating on what to do next, she heard more horses. This time they were riding toward her, not away. She ventured a quick look and saw that it was Joe Peterson, Gimpy, and Harley Fry. She stood up and began waving her arms and shouting at them.

It took them another ten minutes to climb the slope to the overhang.

"Thank God you're here," she said. "Clint is unconscious and losing blood fast."

Joe Peterson bent over Clint and listened to his heart and felt his forehead. "His heart sounds strong enough, but we have to get him to a doctor before he loses too much more blood."

"I tried to plug up the holes the best I could," Calico said. "Oh, Joe, we have to do something quick."

"Stopping the blood loss saved his life, Calico," Joe said. He stood and looked around. "Let's do this. Harley, you ride hard to San Reale and get Doctor Wiggins. Bring him to the ranch as quick as you can get him there. That'll save us some time." He turned to Gimpy. "Gimpy, you scrounge around and see if you can find anything we can use to make a travois. It's kind of bare around here, but maybe we can find something we can throw a blanket over to haul him back to the ranch. Calico, keep that cool cloth on his forehead. He doesn't have any fever, but it might help him."

Tears welled up in her eyes as she watched Harley reach over and gently touch Clint on the shoulder. He then jumped on Jerusalem and galloped away.

"How did you know we were here?" she asked.

"When Harley returned to San Reale, he learned of Clint's difficulty with the shooting at the bank. And to make matters worse, he heard talk that he'd taken you with him as a hostage."

"He didn't take me with him, Joe. It was the other way around. I took him with me. It was my idea from the start. In fact, he argued against me going with him."

"Anyway, Harley beat a trail to the ranch and relayed the story to Mister Holliday. When Gimpy got word of it, he pulled your dad aside and told him he was certain he knew where you'd go. It took all of our persuasive skills to keep Mister Holliday off a horse, but he sent me and Gimpy along with Harley. Old Gimpy was right on target. When we were half a mile away, we could see the dust of the riders leaving."

She stood and gave him a hug. "Thank you, Joe. Thank you so much."

Joe ducked his head and kicked at a rock.

Chapter Forty-Two

Later at the ranch, Doctor Wiggins removed the bullet from Clint's side and patched him up as well as he could. "Rest will do him more good than my prodding around on him," he said to Calico. "I'll be back in a day or so to check on him. In the meantime, keep him comfortable and let nature take its course."

Calico sat with Clint as he lay unconscious in the upstairs bedroom at the Holliday Ranch for three days. During that time, Harley spelled her often, both of them hoping against hope that he would wake up and be his old self again. She sat at his bedside and wiped his forehead, shaved his dark stubble, and kept close watch for any sign that he was going to pull out of his deep sleep.

On a few occasions, she could hear him mumbling, more often than not just a string of incoherent words. But each time gave her more hope.

On the afternoon of the third day, she was sitting beside the bed when Harley came into the room. He took a chair beside her.

"Any change?" he asked.

She shook her head. "None that I can see. He moves from time to time, and still mumbles some. Other than that, he's about the same. Doctor Wiggins said it might take days, or even weeks."

She was quiet for a few minutes, then looked over at Harley. "I know very little about this man, except that he whipped a mountain of a man because of me. You know him better than anyone. Tell me about him."

Harley studied her for a moment, unsure of how to respond. When he had ridden into the ranch with Doctor Wiggins, he'd been quick to recognize it as the ranch where they had left the little blue-eyed girl twelve years ago. He was surprised that Clint hadn't recognized the ranch, but he knew his friend had tried to erase as many of those memories as possible from his mind. The ones he had held on to were those of the little blue-eyed girl. But she had changed so much since then, Harley wasn't surprised that he didn't recognize her.

Later, while Doctor Wiggins was tending to Clint, Gimpy had told him the whole story of the cavalry coming to the ranch, and the excitement of Sarah Holliday when they had left the little girl with them. Calico had changed over the years, of course, as she had grown into a beautiful young woman. Now, all these many years later, their paths had crossed once more. As far as Harley knew, neither Clint nor Calico realized their past connection at the canyon.

But he had an inkling of Clint's feelings toward her—and her feelings toward Clint.

He was unsure of what to say, or how much of Clint's life to reveal to her. He twisted around in the chair and scratched at his gray beard. Talking to females was never his strong suit. But he guessed he would give it a try since she had asked.

"There's one thing I know that's been on Clint's mind fer years," he said. "He mightn't approve of me telling you, but I aim to do it anyways. There's been a girl on his mind he can't shake the memory of. He speaks of her often, sometimes even when he don't even realize it."

He saw Calico lower her head and wipe at her eyes. Then she asked in a shaky voice, "Who was this person, Harley? Why can't he forget her?"

Harley noticed the pained look on her face and hesitated. He immediately regretted that he'd spoken. *I shoulda kept my mouth shut. Why did I think I had the right to tell either of them what happened twelve years ago? It's true the little girl at the canyon had been in Clint's thoughts for years, but it ain't my place to tell her.*

He stood and walked toward the bedroom door. "Ferget I mentioned it, Calico," he said. "Ferget I said anything."

She jumped up and followed him to the door. "Harley, what's wrong? Where are you going?"

But he ran down the stairs without looking back or explaining.

Calico returned to her chair, shocked and hurt by Harley's revelation. Clint had someone else in his life he couldn't forget. She gazed at him and wondered about this other woman. What was she like? How long had he known her?

It was then she remembered how he had reacted at the overhang just a short time ago. How he wouldn't talk about their sudden embrace and kisses. How he had pulled back from her. She now understood why. And she also understood why he wanted to have that *long talk* with her. He had perceived her feelings toward him, and the long talk was going to be his way of letting her down easy.

She put her hands to her face and let the tears flow, as Clint lay in the bed fighting for his life.

CHAPTER FORTY-THREE

On the fourth day, Calico had been dozing on and off in a chair beside Clint's bed. She awoke with a start and jerked her head over at her patient. He was staring at the ceiling, his eyes open wide, but not yet fully alert. She put her hands to her mouth.

"Clint, you're awake!"

He looked at her and smiled, but did not speak.

"Welcome back to the world," she said.

He looked all around the room. "Where am I? What happened?" he asked in a hoarse whisper.

"You were shot twice," she said, as she leaned over the bed. "Once in the side and once alongside your head. We thought you were a goner a time or two, but we never counted on your stubbornness. You lost about a gallon of blood before Doc Wiggins got the holes all plugged up."

"I was scared for a minute that you were an angel when I saw you."

She laughed and relief flooded her whole being. "I've been called many things in my life, by many people, but I don't ever recall being called an angel."

She watched as he touched his head, then his side. Both were covered with thick strips of gauze. He closed his eyes for a moment of rest, then opened them and said, "Am I at your ranch?"

"Yes. And before you ask, you've been in that bed for four days."

"Four days," he whispered. "How did it happen?"

"You and I made a run from San Reale—do you remember that?"

"I remember the bank shooting, and you taking me to Gimpy's hideout in the hills, but not much after that."

Calico related to him what had occurred at the overhang after he had been wounded.

"That's not the first time that old coot has shown up not a minute too soon. And he brought some good help with him."

"You've been sleeping ever since."

Clint motioned her over to the bed and held out his hand. "Thanks for saving my worthless hide, Calico." He then dropped his head back on the pillow and closed his eyes.

Calico sat down beside the bed, still holding on to his hand.

CHAPTER FORTY-FOUR

On the morning of the sixth day after the shooting incident, Clint managed to stumble out of the bedroom without falling on his face. He had one of Justus Holliday's discarded crutches under his left arm. Calico and Harley were seated at the kitchen table eating the morning meal Rosita had prepared. They both jumped up when they saw him leaning against the doorway to steady himself.

"Clint Ramsay, what do you think you're doing?" Calico shouted, while rushing over to grab his arm. "You shouldn't be out of bed."

Harley hurried to her side and took hold of the other arm. "Easy now."

"Easy sounds good right about now, Harley. So does a plate of those eggs and a stack of Rosita's flapjacks."

"Looks like he might be getting back to normal," Harley said.

Rosita was right behind them carrying a huge platter. "I hear you walking about and know you would be hungry, Meester Clint. I was all ready for you."

"Thank you, Rosita."

"Sam Elder is outside with a warrant for your arrest," Calico said. She had taken a seat across the table from him while he feasted. "He badgered Judge Willoughby enough that the judge signed the warrant, even though he has stated in the newspaper that you're in the clear. I have a sneaky feeling that Jake Polk and the banker were in cahoots on a few shady deals, and now

Polk wants you out of the way. You need to be careful with the sheriff, considering the condition you're in. He's been doing a lot of strutting around in that shiny new badge."

"I'm going out to check on the horses," Harley said. "You take care of yourself with the sheriff now, you hear? I'll be close by if things get testy."

Calico sat and watched Clint as he put away half a dozen eggs, a stack of flapjacks, and a beef steak that would choke a horse, along with a pot of black coffee.

"You were on your deathbed less than a week ago, so how can you put away so much food now?"

"Gotta get my strength back. I've got things to do."

When he'd finished the last bite, he tossed aside his napkin and said, "I guess it's time for me to go face the music."

She reached out and grabbed his hand. "Be careful, Clint. I wouldn't want anything to happen between you and the sheriff. There's been enough shooting around here already. It has to stop somewhere."

He looked into her eyes and saw her emotion. She was right. The violence had to stop somewhere, but he knew it wasn't going to be ending anytime soon. There was no other way now that things had gone this far.

"I'll be careful, I promise."

Clint walked out to the veranda where he saw Sheriff Elder standing next to the hitching post. Elder held a piece of paper in his hand. Clint smiled when he saw Joe Peterson, Gimpy, and Harley on three sides of the sheriff, each with a Winchester in his hands pointing carelessly at the sky.

Elder looked around him, coughed, and said, "Uh . . . Ramsay . . . uh . . . the judge . . . uh . . . signed this here warrant for your arrest, but . . . uh . . ." He looked over at Gimpy and Joe, sweat popping out on his forehead. "But . . . uh . . . after considering all the evidence, I . . . I don't think it's necessary to serve it." Elder tore the paper into small pieces, jumped on his horse, and left the ranch in a hurry.

Gimpy let out a horse laugh as Elder raced away from the ranch. "Look at him go. The fastest he has ever moved."

"Will he be back later?" Clint asked. "Or is it all over?"

"It's all over," Joe said. "After you got clean away from the posse, Siena Welborn must have gotten scared and skipped town with all the cash she could get from the bank. No one has been able to locate her since then. And Ernie Teal told the newspaperman how you came to be at the bank in the first place, and how Myron had tried to get Willie to kill you. He put out a special edition that set San Reale right on its ears. Anyway, as far as everyone in San Reale is concerned, not only are you in the clear, they're ready to buy you a round of drinks at the Half-Moon."

Clint nodded. "Thanks, men. I wouldn't be here if not for you." Then he turned to Calico. "And to you, Calico."

When everyone on the porch had scattered, Calico sat down in a rocking chair while Clint stood leaning against a veranda column.

"I think you left out a few details about the shooting at the overhang," Clint said. "Care to tell me why John Henry and Redwing didn't follow through and finish me off when they had the chance?"

"No, I guess I can tell you, although it's not much of a mystery. After they shot you, they thought you were dead, so they started up the slope to make sure. You had dropped your gun, and I saw it near the ledge. I crawled out, got it, and scared them off with a couple of shots. They retreated back down the slope and hid behind the boulder. I guess they thought it was you who was shooting at them."

"If they had only known what I knew," he said, with a laugh.

"Knew what?"

"That they would have been better off if it had been me shooting at them."

CHAPTER FORTY-FIVE

Later that day, Clint was sitting on the veranda drinking a glass of Rosita's tea and watching the activity going on around the ranch. He was thinking of how he would like for his ranch to be just like this one.

Justus Holliday joined him and dropped down in one of the chairs. He fiddled with a tobacco pouch for a few moments, then lit his pipe. "Life gets complicated sometimes when you least expect it doesn't it?" he said.

"What do you mean?" Clint asked.

Justus smiled. "Oh, I see the looks passing between you and Calico. It's not hard for an old man like me to figure things out if given enough time. Don't forget, it happened to me once upon a time. Sarah, bless her heart, was the best thing that ever happened to me. She tamed a bit of my wild blood and gave me reason and hope for the future. Without her, there's no telling what I might have become. Some women have that kind of effect on men. Calico just might be one of them, who knows?"

"It's that obvious, huh?"

"It became pretty obvious to me when she wouldn't leave your bedside during your recovery. She never left your bedside except when it was necessary."

Clint was reluctant to bring up the subject of their overnight stay at Gimpy's hideout, but he felt the need to clear the air. "Mister Holliday, how do you feel about our overnight adventure at Gimpy's hideout?"

"Calico told me all about it. She's a special gal, that Calico. You don't know this about her, but she's not our blood daughter. She came to us when she was nine years old. The cavalry found her after a terrible incident not too far from here. Her folks were killed and the troopers had no way of dealing with her, so they left her with us." Justus leaned forward and added, "She had terrible experiences as a youngster, but Sarah did a remarkable job of helping her get through it."

Clint then understood why he had noticed something about her the first time he saw her. *She's the little girl from the canyon.*

"Go on," Clint said. "I'd like to hear more about her."

"She likes the wide-open spaces, horse riding and her independence," Justus said. "She sees a lot of those traits in you I think. Your need for independence and your self-reliant character among a host of others." Justus laughed and said, "We brought in a tutor from San Antonio when she was about ten years old. The fellow ran her through a tough curriculum for three years, until he said she knew everything he knew and he packed up and left."

Clint remained silent while he thought the situation through. *Should I tell Justus that I was the corporal who found her?* He decided to keep his part in the canyon drama to himself for a time. Visions of the carnage at the canyon that had haunted him for so long reappeared in his mind. He couldn't imagine how a little girl nine years old could rid herself of those images. He couldn't return her to a world of guns and killing that had been his lot in life for so long. She had grown into a special kind of person, and he couldn't take her back to that kind of violent world.

"I can't deny that I feel the same way toward her," Clint said. "But I can't even think about her living in my world. The best thing for both of us would be for me to leave San Reale and the ranch for good as soon as I'm able. I'll go back to Kansas City, and then on to wherever Lucas sends me from there. She'll soon forget all about me."

"We'll see," Holliday said, tapping his pipe on the palm of his hand. "We'll see."

CHAPTER FORTY-SIX

Siena Welborn watched Jake Polk pace the floor of the freight warehouse loft. It was hot under the tin roof, and dusty from the boxes and crates that had been stored there for years. But she couldn't complain since she didn't dare show her face on the San Reale streets. When she saw the futility of trying to convince the people of San Reale that Clint Ramsay had murdered Myron, she ran to Jake Polk for help. She had seen how he'd looked at her on the streets and knew what that look meant. She hadn't been mistaken. He had welcomed her with open arms.

Siena had found Myron's hidden stashes of money at their home soon after his death. Then, after dark on that same day, she had taken Myron's spare set of keys and cleaned out all the available cash at the bank. All told, she now had over seven thousand dollars in her possession.

But she didn't tell Jake Polk of her windfall. That was going to be her little secret.

"I'll get you out of here after dark," Polk said. "There's a place outside of town where you can hide."

"But then what? I can't stay around here after that story I made up about Ramsay killing Myron. I found a few dollars of Myron's money, but that won't be enough to last forever."

Polk laughed. "Siena, you stick with me and you'll be swimming in money." He then told her all about the plan he had in the works. The more he talked, the more excited she became.

This was what she had been waiting for all her life: wealth, pretty clothes, bright lights, and big cities. Then she remembered that Myron had promised her those things as well, but his promises disappeared like a tumbleweed in a dust storm after the *I dos* were said.

She would play this opportunity for all it was worth. If it didn't work out, well, she still had Myron's stash to fall back on.

"Come on, Jake, let's go after the gold now. Why wait? You said everything is ready. We have a dead sheriff and a dead banker on our hands. Pretty soon someone is going to start asking questions. Like the Rangers. Why wait any longer?"

"You're right," he said. "The problem is with the man who dreamed up this deal. He's a cautious man: a goody, goody kinda man. I've been waiting on him to tell me it's time to go, but he always has one more detail to work out. But from now on, we'll do it the Jake Polk way—the Colonel William Clarke Quantrill way—go in hard and fast, shoot anybody who gets in the way, and then get the hell outta town. Can you live with that?"

"I can live with it easy enough, but what about this detective Ramsay? I hear he's back on his feet at the Holliday Ranch. Aren't you scared that he'll call in the Rangers?"

"Don't worry about the Rangers. The Underwoods are not about to let someone else come in and take credit for their work. It's us against Ramsay and that old man. I like the odds."

He pulled her closer to him and said, "When we're finished here we can head for New Orleans in style together—you and me. Nobody will know us there, and they won't give a damn where our money came from either. New Orleans. That's the town, Siena. We'll take that town in style."

"One more day for a share of half a million dollars," she said, throwing up her hands. "Wheeee."

"Or more, maybe," he said. He pulled her even closer to him and kissed her, then whispered in her ear, "Remember, when all is said and done, it's you, me, and New Orleans."

CHAPTER FORTY-SEVEN

On the eighth morning, Clint declared himself fit. He walked out on the porch not long after sunup and stretched his arms high over his head. The pain was gone. Now it was time to finish the job he and Harley had started. He'd had plenty of time to think it over while lying in bed. Things had begun to look clearer to him as he thought about all that had occurred. Someone, he didn't know who, but someone had their sights on a major operation. All the signs pointed to it: Ed Wilhoit had been killed because he knew something; he and Harley had been bushwhacked because Ed had asked them for help; and Marva and Welborn had been killed to stop them from talking. Then he and Calico had been trailed and ambushed by two known killers.

But now, thanks to Harley, he knew where they had set up their headquarters: an old abandoned homestead. It was time that he and Harley wiped out that nest of vipers. But he still didn't know what was going on. John Henry Lockhart and Redwing were the out-front gunmen, but who was the brains behind the outfit? Jake Polk?

And that mysterious message from Wilhoit still nagged at him: *You are involved.* He was no closer to figuring out what that meant than when he started. Still, the homestead sounded like a good starting place.

While he was mulling over the particulars, Justus approached him holding a piece of paper. He handed it to Clint. "I found

175

this note nailed to the barn door this morning. It's addressed to you."

The paper was folded with his name written on the outside. He unfolded it and read it aloud: "*Meet me at the mission around dusk.* Anyone see who put the note on the door?" Clint asked.

"No. We just have a skeleton crew here since all the others are away driving a herd to Fort Kilpatrick. Whoever did it was as quiet as a sun lizard. What're you going to do? It could be some kind of a trap, you know."

"It could be."

"If you're going to the mission, let me and Harley go along with you—just in case."

"Thanks, Justus," he answered. "But I think I'd better handle this alone. It appears this person doesn't want to be seen, so I'll play along with him for the time being."

Clint left the ranch riding Buck two hours before dark. He rode easy and slow, listening to the sounds and watching everything around him. He was sticking to the road that led to Saint Anthony's Mission, stopping often to check both his back trail and the trail in front of him. When he was still half a mile from his destination, a man on horseback appeared out of the brush. The man stopped in the middle of the road in front of him. Clint let his hand rest on the butt of his Colt and watched the man in the approaching darkness. As he got closer, Clint recognized the rider and relaxed.

The man motioned him forward. Clint followed along the road behind the man to a small adobe hut. They both dismounted and faced each other.

"Father Matthew," Clint said. "This is a surprise." The other time he'd seen Father Matthew was on his visit to the small mission his second day in the area.

"Thanks for coming," Father Matthew said. "I apologize for being so mysterious, but I'm afraid it was necessary at this point." Father Matthew invited him inside and pointed him to a wooden stool. He poured them each a cup of coffee then sat on a wooden bench facing Clint.

"Mister Ramsay, I think I need to explain a few things. Some of this you might have already surmised, but some of it might surprise you. A couple things I tell you might even confuse you."

"I'm ready to listen."

"Many of the things I would *like* to tell you, I cannot repeat, of course, due to the Sanctity of Confession. So, I'll tell you what I can. Ed Wilhoit used to visit me just to talk—kind of man-to-man. Right before he was killed, he told me that a man had come to see him with a get-rich scheme. At first it sounded good to Ed, even plausible. Then, as he began to learn more about the plan, Ed tried to back out. He said it was against all his principles to do what they wanted him to do."

"Did he elaborate?"

"Somewhat. They wanted Ed to take several men to Massacre Canyon."

"Massacre Canyon? Why?"

"Well, Ed kind of brought it on himself, I'm afraid. He had talked to a few close friends about the slaughter at the canyon, and how he'd been there and had seen the aftermath. Of course, it didn't take long for everyone to know Ed's story. The men who approached him are after a cache of gold they say is hidden in that canyon. They thought Ed could lead them to the right spot since it was common knowledge that he'd been there."

Clint straightened up on the stool at Father Matthew's statement. "Not that hogwash about gold in that canyon again, Father. There wasn't any gold there: I was there. Take my word for it, there was no gold there, end of discussion."

"Listen to me, Clint, if I might call you that. You may well be correct, but then again, you might not know everything that happened in that canyon."

"If you are referring to the old rumor that the Mexican bandits who were killed in the canyon were carrying stolen gold, I don't believe a word of it. I know books have been written about it, and that speculators have spent their last dollar looking for it. But there's no gold anywhere around that canyon, at least not the kind that was stolen."

Clint talked on and gave his opinion, much of it intense and heated. When he finished, Father Matthew held out his hands in a pleading manner. "Will you listen to me for a few minutes with an open mind? That's all I ask. If you still have doubts afterwards, fine. You can ride away with no harm done. You've ridden out here, so how much difference can a few more minutes of your time make?"

"But it can't be true, Father. I was there. There wasn't any gold in that canyon."

He watched as Father Matthew's head dropped in obvious disappointment. Clint stood and turned toward the door, then stopped and retraced his steps. "All right, Father, I've come this far. I might as well be entertained now that I'm here."

He sat back down on the stool and motioned for Father Matthew to continue.

"Thank you," Father Matthew said. "I don't think you'll be disappointed."

Chapter Forty-Eight

Father Matthew rose from his seat and walked to the door of the hut. He was gone for a few minutes, then returned with a slim Mexican man and an old Indian. The Mexican man had a stooped-over posture with short gray hair and deep brown eyes. He must have been around fifty years old, or at least he looked it. He wore a plain white cotton shirt and brown pants that Clint guessed had been given to him by the father. The Indian looked older than the Mexican, but was shorter, with needle-thin arms and legs. He wore his gray hair in braids that hung down across each shoulder. From his dress, Clint could tell the old man was a Comanche. He could also tell that the Indian was a man of some stature from the way the Mexican deferred to him with every gesture.

The leathery-faced Indian remained standing in the doorway as he looked at Clint.

Clint stared back at him for a moment before he realized who it was standing in front of him: Wolf Eye. He resisted the urge to pull his Colt and right a multitude of wrongs with one well-placed bullet. How many times had he chased this scoundrel and never caught him? Now he was standing within two feet of him.

Wolf Eye looked at him with an unwavering stare. He pointed at Clint's right leg. "Your leg is healed from my arrow?"

Clint was surprised at the question. "It was you who put the arrow in my leg at the creek long ago?"

179

"That is so. I meant to slow you down," he said. Wolf Eye then walked over and put his hand over Clint's heart. "I could have put the arrow here. But I did not want to kill such a brave man."

Clint had always wondered how he had survived that charge at Frenchman's Creek all those years ago. Now he knew.

"Why are you not with your mother's people, and your warrior brothers?" Clint asked. "Why are you living here alone among the white men?"

Wolf Eye waved his hand toward the vast plains surrounding them. "This is where I lived, this is where I will die. Many of my people's bones are scattered among the rocks and hills from the white man's diseases, and from our enemies' weapons. I will join them when it is time. I will not leave my homeland for the white man's reservation."

It seemed that Wolf Eye had eluded capture, as did a few other roving bands of Comanches. For the most part, their reign of terror was over and the majority of them lived in the Kiowa/Comanche reservation at Fort Sill, Oklahoma. But a few still wandered off in search of the old ways.

Father Matthew motioned for the two men to sit beside him on the bench facing Clint.

"For your information, Clint, these two men have been living in a hut in our village for some time. I assure you, they are peaceful men. Due to my sacred vows, I couldn't say anything about this to anyone unless they were willing to speak of their own free will."

Clint nodded, but didn't speak. He would bide his time and make up his own mind about the two men. Meanwhile he'd told Father Matthew he would listen, so he was prepared to do just that.

"I want you to hear what these men have to say," Father Matthew said. He looked at the Mexican man. "This man has been reluctant to tell his story to anyone. He's ashamed of his part in the things he's about to tell you, but after I explained what has been occurring in this area, and whose lives are at stake, he has agreed to speak to you."

"I'll listen," Clint repeated.

The Mexican lowered his head then looked at Father Matthew, who nodded his head. "Go on with your story."

"I will tell it as I remember it. You must then make your own conclusions."

CHAPTER FORTY-NINE

The Mexican began speaking: "I was driving the wagon in which the young girl the *banditos* called Little One was riding. She was young, perhaps eight or nine years old. She was a scared little girl and I tried to comfort her as well as I could. For the first three days, she cried herself to sleep each night. Then her tears dried up and she just sat there, frightened.

"I was kind to her, gave her food and water, and combed her hair at night. But I still kept close watch on her every movement. The boss *bandito* was a huge man named Luta Blanca and I was scared of him, I am ashamed to say. When he took the little girl, he killed her father and mother right in front of their burning cabin, right in front of her.

"I shudder to remember how Luta looked at Little One with a wicked smile on his black, greasy-bearded face. He could not wait to get her to Chihuahua to offer her for sale to the rich *senors*. She would bring him many pesos.

"I was worried about a Comanche attack. My wife was of The People, and I feared them. The rocks and boulders made the canyon a perfect place for the Comanche warriors to set a trap. Some said Wolf Eye was in a far-off place called Oklahoma, but I refused to believe it. I would not relax until we were through that hellhole of a canyon. It was the first time I had gone on such a journey, and I knew it would be my last. Never had I imagined how men could be so cruel, so violent. I wanted it to be over. And if I could somehow get Little One away from these *banditos*, I might be able to forgive myself for my part in the treachery.

"Then it happened. I heard a blood-curdling scream. I looked to my left and saw a short, stumpy *bandito*, the one they called Gomez, tumble from his horse with an arrow in his chest. Then I heard more shrill cries of the Comanche raiders as they spilled out of the rocks, overtaking the outriders first, then the mule skinners. From the mouth of the canyon came a dozen thundering horsemen, their faces painted in black, vermilion, and yellow stripes. A few of the warriors fired rifles, but arrows rained down so thick on us from the rocks that the sun was almost blocked. After the warriors had killed the stunned, unprepared outriders, the mule skinners began fleeing in every direction in panic and disarray. They were no match for the Comanche warriors.

"I was frozen in fear, but I pulled Little One up into my arms and tried to get into the rocks. Before I could reach the rocks, a young warrior jumped at me from a ledge. I doubled over to protect the little girl and covered her with my body. He looked at me, and instead of plunging a lance into my chest, he hit me in the head with the butt of his rifle. I remembered no more of the attack.

"Later, when I awakened, my head throbbed, and I was dizzy. But where was I? How had I survived? Looking around, I found that I was in a small cave. I lay still and listened. Outside all was quiet. Then I heard a soft murmuring. Crouched near me I saw Little One, her knees drawn up to her chin. Her eyes were wide and blank. I stumbled over to her and took her by the hand.

"I told her we were safe, to make no sounds. I managed to get to the edge of the cave and looked out at the canyon below. Dead bodies lay all around. The mules and horses that did not survive the attack were already beginning to putrefy in the heat of the desert sun. The stock that did survive was long gone.

What remained of the freight wagons and the mule packs were scattered along the canyon floor. Vultures were everywhere.

"I gave Little One a hug and pointed to a spot at the rear of the cave. 'Stay right here, Little One,' I said. 'Don't go anywhere. I'll be back.' She moved to the back of the cave and sat down as instructed. She lowered her head into her arms and began to cry. I watched her with a heavy heart and repeated, 'I'll be back, Little One.'

"I managed to maneuver down through the rocks to the wreckage. I saw Quintas, and Antonio, and Pecos. And under a wrecked wagon I saw the body of Luta Blanca. All dead. I fell to my knees and sobbed. Then I pulled myself up and walked among the dead bodies seeking life, but I found none.

"Then I tripped over one of the leather packs the mules had carried. I kicked at it in anger, then again and again. I fell exhausted on the pack. As I did, I saw the bright yellow rocks fall from a leather pack. I open it and found many, many more of them. I shuffled to another pack and found more yellow rocks, and then another, and another. In the last pack I found a shiny gold cross covered with sparkling jewels of all colors, and gold cups, and a gold candlestick holder. Now I understood why Luta had wanted to stop at the old mission.

"He had stolen these objects from the mission! I was stunned at the sight of all the yellow rocks. I knew what they were. But most of all, I was repelled at the sight of the holy objects. Sacrilege! Calling on all the strength I could muster, I set to work to hide the packs of plunder while Little One slept.

"I had almost finished my work when I heard horses and saw that it was American soldiers. That is when I took Little One down to where I was sure she could be found by the soldiers."

★ ★ ★ ★ ★

Clint sat there speechless, trying to absorb what he'd heard. He looked from the storyteller to Father Matthew, then to Wolf Eye.

"This is incredible," he said to Father Matthew. "Do you believe him? Can this preposterous tale be true?"

Wolf Eye held up his right hand. "What Elizano says is spoken from the heart. It is true."

Elizano! That's what Calico was shouting when he first spotted her at the canyon. She was shouting for this man who had cared for her in the midst of all the butchery. Elizano!

Then Wolf Eye told him what happened while Elizano was unconscious: "My warriors were herding the horses and mules. I heard Horned Owl shout. He pointed to a man on the ground. It was Elizano, a man who had taken my daughter as his wife. Elizano was kind to her, and had visited us. We carried him to a cave known to the Comanche. We washed his head wound and tended to him as well as we could without proper herbs. I saw that the little girl was special to him because of his protective ways. We had no use for the white man's gold. We left it. We left water for Elizano and the girl then rode away. The men with blue coats were not far behind us. It would have been foolish of us to remain any longer."

It was true after all. There had been gold at that canyon.

"One more thing, then you will know everything that I know," Father Matthew said. "Yesterday a young Mexican man came to the mission. He had been sleeping out in the open without any food. He told me that he'd been hired as a mule skinner by some *gringos.* He said he'd been mistreated and had to run away from them. Then he said that he understood some Texican words, and heard the men talk about what they were going to do when they got the girl, and she took them to the canyon to get the gold."

Father Matthew threw up his hands. "That's why I left the message for you. Do you have any idea what the mule skinner was talking about?"

Clint did indeed understand what the mule skinner was saying, but he didn't have time to explain it to Father Matthew. He ran out the door, jumped on Buck and left the mission at a gallop.

He also understood now what Ed Wilhoit had meant by: *You are involved.*

CHAPTER FIFTY

Clint pushed Buck as hard as he dared to in the darkness. The territory through which he was riding was not all that familiar to him, so he couldn't go all out as he wanted. Still, he had to get back to the ranch as fast as possible to warn Justus Holliday. He was ticking off the minutes in his head as he slapped at Buck's flanks.

"Come on, boy, we can make it. Come on, Buck, push."

He guessed it had taken him close to two hours to ride to the priest's hut. He had ridden in no particular hurry at the time, so now, with Buck going all out, he should be able to reach the ranch in half of that amount of time even in the dark.

Buck was still running hard when he reached the arched entrance to the ranch. Clint slowed him to a walk while he scanned the area in front of him. He didn't want to ride into another ambush. There were lights glowing in the main house, but the bunkhouse was dark. The two hands who had remained at the ranch and had missed the cattle drive must not have returned yet.

He relaxed. Everything seemed to be normal. He rode up to the house, dismounted and tied Buck to the hitching post. He paused at the veranda and scanned the ranch once again, not seeing anything that bothered him.

Calico came to the door. "It's about time you showed up," she said. "We were about to round up Harley to go out to look for you."

He grabbed her by the shoulders and pushed her into the house. "We have to talk. Is your father still up?"

"What's the matter, Clint? You look so—"

"Go get your father, Calico. Hurry."

Calico backed away from him, and ran to her father's room. She was back in two minutes, supporting Justus on her shoulder.

"What's this all about, Clint? Has something happened?"

"I know why those men have been watching the ranch, and I know what they're after," he said. "It's Calico they're after."

"They're after Calico? Why in thunderation would they be after Calico?"

Before Clint could answer, the front door slammed open and a man stood there with a gun pointed in their direction.

"I'll tell you why, old man. That purty little gal knows something that she aims to tell the rest of us. Ain't that right, little gal?"

Clint's greatest fear had come to life when he saw John Henry Lockhart standing in the doorway.

CHAPTER FIFTY-ONE

Jake Polk brushed by John Henry and pointed for everyone to sit on the floor. "Down, everybody. On the floor. Get Ramsay's gun, John Henry, and search the others for weapons. Then search the house and see if there's anyone else here." Turning to his captives, he said, "Now listen, all of you. You do as I say and no one will be harmed. You do something crazy, like trying to run, then John Henry here has orders to shoot."

While Polk talked, another man came into the room. Clint recognized him as the man who had sided John Henry on the trail—the man called Redwing. His face was covered with streaks of dried blood, and splotches of deep red cuts.

"Two cowhands come," Redwing said. "Go to bunkhouse."

He spotted Clint on the floor and looked down at him. "You cheat death again. We miss you in hills. Different this time."

"Looks like we didn't miss you," Clint said.

Redwing kicked him in the ribs and put a hand to his own face. "I kill you for this."

John Henry came back into the room and looked around. He turned to another man. "Where's that old man who rides with Ramsay? He's ain't in here."

"Not in bunkhouse," Redwing said.

Polk walked over to Clint and said, "Where's Fry?"

"Why ask me? I'm not his keeper. He goes where he wants, when he wants. If he wasn't in the bunkhouse, then I'd guess he took a big thirst to the Half-Moon. He gets that way sometimes.

189

If I'm not mistaken, he'll come staggering in sometime tomorrow with a big headache."

"Get on back and watch the bunkhouse, Redwing. If he shows up, you know what to do with him." Polk turned to Justus. "Come with me, Holliday. You're going to tell the cowpunchers that you and the lady of the house are going on a business trip and not to worry about you. You had better be real convincing, or you might regret what happens to them. Just make sure they stay calm and don't bother us."

Polk and Justus returned a few minutes later with Polk grinning. "Holliday here missed his calling. He oughta been an actor—like one of them Booths. Those cowpunchers won't be bothering us." He then grinned at Clint and said, "I'm going to take great pleasure in shooting you. I oughta do it right now in front of everybody, but I'll wait until we get away from the ranch. I don't want to raise any suspicions among those cowpokes. It seems you have a habit of interfering in our business a little too often. But let me assure you, this will be the last time you interfere with me."

Polk went to the door and spoke to someone standing outside. Clint couldn't make out what he said, but a few seconds later, the banker's wife and a man he didn't know walked into the room. A few minutes later, he heard Polk refer to him as Hocker.

The banker's wife looked much different this time. Instead of the lavish clothes he had seen her wearing at the Cattlemen's Bank, she was wearing riding pants, a man's tan flannel shirt, and fashionable brown boots. She looked around the room and saw Clint stretched out on the floor clutching at his ribs where Redwing had kicked him.

"You should be dead, Ramsay," she said. "You can't say I didn't try my best. But then, you said we'd be seeing each other again. I guess you're one of those prophets the preachers are always shouting about."

"I'll give you due credit for your efforts. You almost pulled it off. Almost."

"No, I did pull it off. Look around you. You're the one on the floor gasping for breath, not me."

Polk pulled Hocker aside and they talked in low voices. Clint could tell by their glances they were talking about him. *Not good,* he thought.

"Listen up," Polk said. "All of you move over there near the side wall and sit down with your backs against the wall. Easy now, no quick moves. Tie Ramsay's hands and feet, John Henry. Don't bother with the girl or the old man just yet." Polk sat down backwards in a straight-back chair, his arms draped on the chair's back. He appeared calm and sure of himself. "Let me tell you what we're going to do. Like I said, you cooperate and nobody gets hurt. You don't cooperate, well . . . no promises on that account. Hocker here and the other two have orders to keep things quiet and under control. Anyone who disagrees with that will suffer the consequences."

"Take the cattle if that's what you're after," Holliday said. "Take them and be damned."

"Oh, you can keep your cattle, old man. We're after something a little more substantial than longhorns, and you're going to help us find it."

"You won't find it here," Holliday replied. "There's a couple hundred dollars in the safe, but that's all. But take it and leave us alone."

"Tell him what we're after, little lady," Polk said, looking over at Calico.

"I don't know what you're talking about," she said.

"I expected that from you, so let me explain how it's going to be. We're going to that place they call Massacre Canyon where you were found by the army. You're going to show us the hiding place of that gold. When we get the gold in our hands, we leave the country and you go back to your routine, boring lives. It's that simple. If you refuse, we think we have ways to convince you to reconsider."

"I was just a little girl back then," Calico said. "I have no idea where that place is, or how to get to it. Furthermore, I don't know anything about a stash of gold. You have to believe me, because it's the truth. I never saw any gold."

Polk stood and kicked the chair out of his way. "It's getting late. Maybe in the morning your memory will be better. But remember this when you go to bed tonight. Ed Wilhoit got all uppity and refused to cooperate with us, and you know what happened to him. So you might dream about that tonight."

Polk turned to the banker's wife. "Siena, you go with the Holliday woman and keep an eye on her. John Henry, you had better tie the Holliday woman's hands and feet. I wouldn't want her to start getting rowdy with Siena tonight. I hear she can be a real hellion sometimes. Ramsay, you and the old man . . . well, just do the best you can under the circumstances."

CHAPTER FIFTY-TWO

Polk gathered everyone into the main room the following morning at sunrise. He appeared to be well rested and eager to get on with the task at hand. His face had darkened underneath his heavy brows, and he spat out orders all around. He had traded his usual businessman's attire for cotton pants and a blue shirt with pearl-like buttons. A leather gun belt circled his waist with an ivory-handled Colt peeking out the top. Overnight he had transformed himself from a businessman to an outlaw.

"We have some long rides in front of us for the next few days," Polk said. "I'll repeat what I said last night. You people cooperate and you'll be fine. If you don't, then all bets are off."

He walked over to where Calico sat. "How about you, little lady? Did your memory improve overnight?"

Calico raised her chin high and said, "I told you I don't know where that place is. I've spent my whole life trying to forget about it."

"Well, don't trouble yourself too much about helping us get to the canyon. We think we can manage that well enough. After all, I have a half brother who has read all the books that were written about the battle. He's even written one or two of them himself. What do they call it? The Lost Massacre Canyon Gold? It's too bad none of those writers or prospectors were able to find your little hiding place though. That's why you're going with us."

"Don't you think if I knew where there was a treasure chest

of gold, I would've gone after it myself long before now? You need to use a little common sense here, mister. I'll tell you for the final time, I don't know anything about any gold in that place."

"You've said that before. But maybe you know more than you think you know."

"Leave her alone," Clint said. "She told you she doesn't know where the place is."

John Henry walked over to Clint with a grin on his face. He grabbed Clint by the front of his shirt with his left hand and lifted him off the floor. With his right hand closed in a tight fist he threw a short jab that jarred him down to his toes. John Henry released him and Clint fell to the floor, dazed but conscious.

"He won't be interrupting you for a while, Jake. Go on with your spiel."

Calico let out a startled cry and tried to run over to him, but Polk pulled her back. "Now, now girl, that's just a sample of what you're going to see if you don't start cooperating more. You or your father could be next."

The front door flew open and Tay Redwing ran into the room and pointed toward the ranch entrance. "A rider."

"Let him come," Jake said. "We'll invite him in."

Within a few minutes there was a knock at the door. Polk opened the door and said, "Come in, come in. We've been expecting you."

Robert Shorter entered the room carrying a brown leather bag. Jake waved his hand around the room and said, "Take a good look, little brother. It went off better than we expected."

Shorter was wearing thick eyeglasses and was smoking a pipe. He looked more like a professor than an outlaw. He turned to Jake and said, "I think everything's in place. Good work."

"You're right on time, Robert," Anse Hocker said from the

corner of the room. "Everything around here is running like a fine watch. We'll be ready to hit the trail in half an hour. You got all your maps and information?"

"I believe we're ready to go," Shorter said. "I'm confident the Holliday girl can lead us right to the gold once we get to the canyon. Here, let me show you men what I have."

Clint was woozy from John Henry's punch, but he fought to keep his wits about him. He gave a quick glance at the four men who were immersed in their conversation. They were not paying any attention to him. He let out a soft whistle and got Calico's attention. When she looked his way, he made a motion for her to move over closer to him.

She got the message and scooted across the floor to where he lay.

"Clint, what are we going to do? That other man that came in, this Shorter. He thinks I can show him the location of the gold. These men scare me."

Clint then remembered where he had seen Shorter before. He was the painter who had set up his studio at Martha Ann's Boardinghouse. Another thought came to mind. The colorful paintings on the covers of Ed Wilhoit's dime novels were too similar to Shorter's paintings to be coincidental. This man's name might be Robert Shorter, but Clint was certain the man wrote his books under the name of Bison Bob.

Clint leaned in close to her and spoke in a low whisper. "Calico, these men scare me, too, so we have to play along and not do anything we might regret. I think I know how to buy us some time. You're going to hear something in a few minutes that might surprise you. You just go along with me. Don't say anything, just let me do the talking. Can you do that for me?"

"For you? Of course I can. We still have to have that long talk, remember?"

His hands were tied behind his back, and he was light-headed, but he managed to get to his feet. He leaned against the wall for support. "Polk," he shouted. "Come over here. We need to talk."

Jake Polk looked over at him. "I'm through talking to you, Ramsay. If you do any talking, it had better be you saying your prayers. Your time on this earth is about to end. I don't have the time or the inclination to deal with you. You're excess baggage now."

"I wouldn't be so hasty if I were you. I want to make a deal with you."

Polk laughed. "Look at you. All trussed up like a pig ready for slaughter. What kind of deal can you make with me?"

"You don't need Calico to take you to the gold. I can take you."

CHAPTER FIFTY-THREE

Clint was still leaning against the wall when Polk walked over to him. He grabbed Clint by the chin and jerked his head upwards. "Say that one more time, Detective. I'm not sure I heard you right the first time."

Robert Shorter, Hocker and John Henry also heard what he had said and joined Polk.

Clint glanced in Calico's direction and saw her put her hands to her mouth and shake her head at him. He gave her an almost-imperceptible smile as he spoke. "I said I'll make a deal with you. If you let these people go, I'll take you to the gold. I know the spot you're looking for."

"Start explaining yourself," Shorter said, stepping in front of Polk. "And you had better make it real convincing."

"Yeah," Polk said. "Because like the lady said, if she knew where it was, she'd already have it. That applies double to you."

Clint knew that making a deal with these men was out of the question, but like he told Calico, a good story might buy them time; time enough for an opportunity to present itself. His mission now was to convince them that he could do what he said he could do.

"Which one of you am I dealing with?" Clint asked. "Who's giving the orders around here?"

Shorter tapped Clint on the chest. "This is my play. I make the decisions. Now you have one last chance to explain yourself, or I'll let my brother take care of you in his own way. I don't like violence, but Jake here kind of likes it."

Clint looked at Polk. "So you're really Jake Shorter, are you?" he said. "You changed your name like all those other killers who rode with Quantrill, and are now hiding. If I'd ridden with that killer, I would've changed my name, too."

Polk backhanded him and said, "Don't say nothing bad about the colonel."

Clint staggered, but stayed on his feet.

"Now start explaining," Robert Shorter said.

"You go by the name of Bison Bob when you write those books, don't you?" Clint asked. "You're the man who wrote all those stories about Massacre Canyon and the lost gold?"

"Yes, and they turned out to be quite successful, too. But what has that got to do with anything?"

"I'd place a wager that you were the man who dragged Ed Wilhoit into this scheme. Am I right?"

Shorter nodded. "That's very astute of you, Detective. Ed had some strange scruples that gold couldn't overcome. He became a danger to us, and Jake here had to . . . well . . . let's say we couldn't take a chance on him spoiling our well-planned endeavor."

Clint nodded. "I thought as much. As for your well-planned endeavor, if you know that Calico Holliday was the little girl at the canyon, the sole survivor of the bloody Indian massacre, then you must know that she was found by a trooper of the US cavalry. Right?"

"Go on," Shorter said.

"That someone was me. I was the corporal with the Third Cavalry who found her among the rocks that day."

He heard a gasp from Calico, but resisted the urge to look at her. He had to keep his attention focused on Shorter, the one person he had to convince that he could be useful to them, otherwise . . .

Shorter walked over to his leather case and dug around in it. When he found what he was searching for, he returned to Polk's side. He held out a sheet of paper and pointed at it. "My research shows there was a Corporal Ramsay riding with the Third Cavalry at Massacre Canyon on that day. And I have learned from my inquiries that it was indeed a corporal who found her in the rocks. But there are no Christian names. What he's telling us could be true."

"Do we have a deal, Shorter? I'll agree to take you to the exact location where I found Calico, and you let the Hollidays go free. You know she was too young to remember anything about the canyon. One rock will look like any other rock to her. You need me at the canyon, not her."

Clint could see that Shorter was thinking it over, so he pushed harder. "You believe the gold can't be hidden too far from where I found her. That's why you've gone to all this trouble to get her. Isn't that right?"

Shorter took the pipe out of his mouth and said, "Yes, that's my belief. The gold must be near where the girl was found."

"Then it's me you need, not Calico." He ventured a look over at Calico and saw tears glistening in her eyes. He gave her a smile, which she returned with a smile of her own.

CHAPTER FIFTY-FOUR

"I'll not make a deal with you," Shorter said. "But I might be persuaded to take you along to see if you can make good on your promise. If we get the gold, then you live. If you fail to lead us to the gold, big brother Jake will deal with you in his own particular way. How's that for a deal?"

Clint knew further discussion was useless, but he also knew he'd bought himself a day or two in which to act. Now he had to be on the lookout for his opportunity. One would offer itself, of that he was certain. He just had to be on watch for it.

"I'll take you to the gold, but Calico and her father stay here. You don't need them with me along."

Jake Polk jumped into the conversation at this juncture. "No, I think she just might provide some incentive for you to co-operate. You two have become pretty chummy these last few days. No, Justus and Calico go with us as planned. I don't think we'll have any problems from you with them along. You fail to cooperate with us and those two people are liable to get hurt."

Clint glanced over at Calico once more and winked. It hurt him to see the terror in her eyes, so he managed a smile for her benefit.

Jake Polk herded them all into the front yard. The sun was an hour up, and travel time was wasting. Robert Shorter was standing beside him, looking uncomfortable in high-top boots, denim pants and a red cotton shirt. But he was still chewing on his pipe.

"From this point forward," Shorter said, "I shall turn the matter over to my brother, Jake. He'll be in charge until we reach our destination. I'll lodge myself in the rear of the second wagon where I'll review my notes and be available for advice and consultation. It's quite possible that I'll make a few sketches to memorialize our journey."

He nodded at Jake. "Please take charge."

Polk was eager to get on the trail. His three gun hands were standing beside the wagons with their guns drawn. The mule skinners were busy tightening straps and harnesses for the journey. The two women were standing apart, avoiding each other. Calico was alongside Justus, holding on to his arm, while Siena was leaning against a wagon pulling a comb through her long black hair. Clint, with his hands still tied, was in front of the wagons.

Polk took Calico by the arm. "Get on the seat in the front wagon," he ordered.

"If I have to go with you, I want to ride Dusty, not in a bumpy wagon."

Polk grabbed her by the shoulders and said, "Get in the damn wagon. We'll not be chasing you all over the country on that horse of yours. You'll ride in the wagon like I said. Now get in, or I'll have John Henry throw you in."

She put her hands on her hips and started to say something in response, but relented and let her hands fall to her sides. She climbed onto the seat of the covered wagon beside Siena.

"Come on, sweetie," Siena said. "You never can tell, you might enjoy my company."

Calico crossed her arms tight across her chest and turned her back to her riding companion.

Polk took Justus to the second wagon and helped him climb

aboard, then went over to Ramsay. "You're going to ride one of the horses, Ramsay. I want that gold, but I'm not above putting a bullet in your brisket if you act up."

Clint held out his hands which were still tied. "You've made your point, Polk. I wouldn't want anything to happen to me, or the Hollidays. You have my guns, so you can untie my hands. But I'll give you a piece of advice. You ought to keep my guns handy. You realize we're heading straight into Comanche territory, don't you?"

"I'll untie your hands, but one move that I consider reckless on your part, down you go. As for your guns, I don't think so."

Clint's first and main concern was to figure out how to get himself, Calico, and Justus away from this bunch of cutthroats. He wouldn't be able to do that as long as they were separated, and he had no weapons. His best chance was to be vigilant, and not miss an opportunity should one present itself. He shook his arms to get rid of the pins-and-needles feeling now that his hands were loose. He kept reminding himself to be patient and watch for an opening.

Clint, along with Polk and Anse Hocker, took the lead as they left the Holliday ranch house. Behind them came the covered wagon with Calico seated on the right side of the bench next to Siena. Robert Shorter sat in a wooden chair at the rear of the second wagon which was full of water barrels and supplies, with another of the mule skinners handling the team. Justus was sitting on the bench beside the driver of the second wagon. Skirting the two wagons on either side were Tay Redwing and John Henry Lockhart. A third mule skinner was tending to the mules and packhorses, and dragging up the rear.

Clint had a rough idea of where the pass might be located, but it was just that—a rough idea. Twelve years had passed since he had been there, and when the cavalry troop left the pass, his attention was on the little girl who clung to him. He had never given a thought to returning to that miserable place. But it seemed certain that Shorter had either been to the canyon in earlier days, or had a good grasp of how to get there.

Shorter had given Polk the maps he had gathered over the past few months while he had hatched this scheme. Polk took it upon himself to be the point man on the trek. Clint rode up to side him as the caravan strung out and began their journey.

"One thing puzzles me, Polk. I know of your reputation back when you went by the name of Jake Shorter, but I never connected that name to you until now. And I've heard a little about Hocker and Lockhart. Why would you need people like that for this job? You could've hired men from the Half-Moon Saloon to do this with a whole lot less trouble."

"Insurance, plain and simple. There are other men out there who would like to get their hands on this hoard of gold. Bobby said he knows other men who have spent years researching this incident just like he has. When he stumbled on some old records that revealed several sacks of refined gold had been stolen from the Altaveli Gold Mine three days before the massacre, it all came together for him. That convinced him there was gold out there to be found. Maybe a fortune. And like you said, we're riding straight into Comanche territory. You can't be sure about them. I'm told they travel in and out of the reservations at will. I figure we can't have too much protection."

"So, Robert, or Bobby, as you call him, has convinced you there's gold in the canyon?"

"After listening to his explanation, I'm sure of it. Most of the stories in those dime novels he wrote are pure fiction, but there's some truth mixed in among the fiction. After all, the gold cups and the gold candlestick holder that were stolen from Saint Anthony's Mission by these very same bandits were later returned without explanation. Somebody knows where that stolen gold is located. Bobby came to the conclusion that the little girl you found was *that somebody.* She didn't survive out of pure luck. There was something—or someone—else at play that day in Massacre Canyon."

Clint had to admit that Polk and Shorter had thought the situation out almost exactly like Elizano and Wolf Eye had described it to him. He decided now would be a good time to do a little gardening, a little seed planting. "Do you think you can trust Hocker and these two gun hands when you find the gold? What's to keep them from shooting every one of us and keeping the gold for themselves? You know when you go to bed with rattlesnakes, sometimes you get bit."

"All you have to worry about is getting us to the spot where you found the girl, no more, no less. I'll take care of everything else." With that comment, Jake Polk slapped his horse and rode off far ahead of the wagons.

Clint watched him ride away, but he still hadn't given up hope. He knew something that Jake Polk, Robert Shorter, and all the rest of them didn't know.

CHAPTER FIFTY-FIVE

Harley Fry was several hundred yards behind the Holliday ranch house, standing behind an oak tree when the wagons headed north toward the outlying hills. The previous night he had been rolled up in his blanket in one of the Holliday horse stalls when he heard the wagons roll into the ranch yard. When he eased himself up to the corner of the stable, he saw John Henry and understood right away that the incident they had feared had arrived. Now in the early morning hours, he was still not sure what they were after, but whatever it was, Clint and Calico seemed to be drawing most of their attention. And Jake Polk appeared to be one of the men in charge. Harley put a cut of tobacco in his jaw as he watched Calico step up into a wagon, then Clint mount a horse surrounded by Polk and two more men.

He watched as the wagons left the ranch, unsure of what to do. He had his Colt and his Winchester, but they would be small comfort against their arsenal of guns. And if he cut loose at them now, he might hit Clint or one of the Hollidays. If he rode into San Reale and sent a telegram to either the Rangers or Lucas Underwood asking for help, it would be several days before anyone could get here. As for Sheriff Elder, Harley was not sure he wasn't tied up with Polk and company in some way.

He was thinking this through when he felt a hand on his shoulder. He clenched his fists and turned, ready to react to the threat. As he did so, he looked into the eyes of his old Comanche enemy.

"Wolf Eye," he said, raising his rifle to point it at the Comanche chief.

"Har-lee," Wolf Eye answered.

The two old fighters stared at each other for a minute, then Wolf Eye said, "Come." He turned and began walking away taking short, choppy strides.

Harley followed the warrior, trying hard not to step on the smaller Wolf Eye.

They walked away from the ranch house for several minutes, then Wolf Eye pointed toward a rocky outcropping. "We go there."

They crawled over a pile of fallen rocks and circled the outcropping to the rear where the ground flattened out. Harley was about to ask Wolf Eye where they were going, when he spotted five horses tied to an old leaning cedar tree. He raised his Winchester to his shoulder, but Wolf Eye reached back with a hand and pushed the barrel toward the ground. "Not shoot."

Harley walked out onto the flat ground and stopped. Sitting next to a small smokeless fire was the Holliday cook, Rosita. Across from her was a man he had never seen before, but from his clothing, he figured out who he was. A third man, an older Mexican, was standing near the horses.

"Hello, Father," he said. He then sat down on the ground cross-legged. "What brings you out this way?"

"Clint was meeting with me at the mission and left in a hurry after he heard Elizano and Wolf Eye's story. I was so concerned at his sudden reaction, we followed him, much slower of course, and saw what was happening. Then Rosita joined us and here we are, trying to determine what to do next."

"Eat, Harley," Rosita said. "We have coffee and beans. Not much, but all I could find."

"I reckon I could use a bite," he said. "I could also use an explanation of what's going on around here." He nodded toward Rosita as he ate. "How did you get away?"

She lowered her eyes as she spoke. "I was at the smokehouse when the men came at night. I was not in the house, so they did not see me, and did not think of me."

"Out of sight, out of mind. Must've worked for me, too."

"Elizano is my father," she said. "And Wolf Eye is my grandfather. He came to the mission when he was sick with the fever, because he knew that Elizano and I were nearby and would help him. It was Elizano and I who cared for him, and he never left. The villagers of Saint Anthony accepted my grandfather as one of their own when my father offered him shelter."

Harley was surprised at that bit of information. "Got any idee where these men are going and why?"

"I think I can answer that question," Father Matthew said. "They're going to Massacre Canyon to find gold that's hidden there."

So that's what this furor is all about. Those men have heard the stories of hidden gold and think Calico and Clint can lead them to it. And they're using Justus as a hostage to force them to cooperate. That was a start. At least Harley now knew where they were headed.

Harley stood and said, "I'm going after those wagons and get Clint and the Hollidays away from them somehow."

"Stop," Rosita said. She then pointed to her head. "We need to think. Those men have many guns."

Harley had to admit she had a good point, so he returned to the fire.

"How many hands are left on the ranch?" Father Matthew asked.

"Two. Both are old and crippled. They will be no help," said Rosita.

"Well, looks like it's up to us, then," Harley said.

Chapter Fifty-Six

The lead covered wagon had been lurching along for perhaps two hours when Calico relented and spoke to Siena. "Just how did you get tied up in this crazy scheme?"

"There's no need for you to try to rile me," Siena said. "We're going to be riding together for several days. We might as well make the best of it."

"You still didn't answer my question."

"You might not believe it from what you've seen of me, but I was raised on a hardscrabble farm where the whole family had to work and scrape eighteen hours a day just to put food on the table. Sometimes even that didn't happen. We had flour sacks for dresses, our hands and knees were cracked and bleeding most of the time. We were hungry all of the time. When I got old enough to know there was a life out there much different from the one I was living, I took off in search of it. The nearest town was Waynesboro, so that's where I headed. I was fifteen years old at the time. I kept looking back, expecting my old man to be coming after me with a willow branch, but he never did . . ."

Calico thought she caught a second of regret in Siena's voice that her father didn't try to stop her.

"Looking back on it, I guess they were glad there was one less mouth to feed. I had three older brothers and two younger sisters. Anyway, at Waynesboro, I managed to survive by working in a leather shop for room and board and a few pennies a day. Then, out of desperation, I threw my pride aside and latched on to a drummer who was passing through town. I stuck with him until we got to Austin, then I slipped away from him. You can guess the rest. I made a vow to myself that I would never live like that again, ever. I don't care what it takes, or who has to get hurt in the doing, I'll not live like that again."

"So now we have a dead sheriff, a dead bushwhacker, and a dead banker. I wouldn't be at all surprised if there aren't many more of us dead before this is all over. And in the midst of this, all you can think of is yourself."

Siena drew back her hand to slap Calico, but stopped. "How would you like to have somebody like Myron Welborn pawing all over you every day? I thought he was my ticket to a life of happiness, but he was just like the others. All he wanted was a pretty girl on his arm to do his bidding, to be at his beck and call. You haven't been where I've been, so stop judging me."

"No, Siena, I haven't been where you've been, but I can tell you there are worse things in life than wearing flour sacks and missing a meal or two. Take it from me, there are worse things. You haven't been where I've been either."

Calico turned away from her seat mate thinking about Siena's life. She wondered how her own life might have turned out if not for the Mexican raiders. Their lives sounded similar up to that point, then Fate had intervened and taken them in drastically different directions. Would she have had the courage to walk away from the . . . What did Siena call it? The hardscrabble farm? But Calico knew that once a person started running away, the running never stopped. She looked over at Siena and guessed that she would be running and searching for that elusive perfect dream for the rest of her life.

The caravan progressed at a steady pace that first day on the trail, stopping twice at streams to water their horses and mules, and once to eat a quick meal of jerky and biscuits they'd brought with them. As they moved farther north, the grass thinned and the terrain became more difficult for the wagons to maneuver on the rocky, rough landscape.

Clint looked back often to see how Calico was holding up. Each time he glanced at her, she would manage a smile for him. He could tell the rough wagon ride over ground that wasn't meant for wagon travel was taking its toll on the two women— and probably Justus in the other wagon. He scanned the horizon in front of him. The ground seemed to be less rocky to the west of the direction in which they were traveling. He pulled his horse to a stop and made a show of looking in all directions. He put his hands over his eyes to shield the sun and said to Polk, "I think we need to veer west more and head toward that tallest mesa. Check your map."

Polk pulled out the map, studied it for a moment, and then motioned for Hocker to join him. The two of them huddled for a brief conversation while Polk made gestures at the map. Then he waved his arm toward the west and shouted at the wagon drivers, "Toward that highest mesa."

Clint breathed a sigh of relief. He had thought that maybe, just maybe, he could run a bluff on Jake Polk. That one worked, so maybe he could pull off another one somewhere down the line if need be.

CHAPTER FIFTY-SEVEN

Clint was becoming weary. All the aches and pains he had taken over the past week weren't leaving as fast as he would have liked. He couldn't remember a time when he had been battered, shot at, and bloodied more than this. Still, he had to bear up and stay alert; others were depending on him.

It was closing in on dark when Jake Polk spotted a stand of trees off to his left, maybe a half mile from where they were riding. He pointed in that direction, and shouted, "Head for those willows and cottonwoods over that way."

Clint thought it was a wise move. The horses were about done in with the heat, and most likely, there was water for the animals to be found somewhere among the trees. It would be a good place to rest up the stock for an early start tomorrow.

Clint smiled as he watched Polk trudge along in front of the wagons. The outlaw looked dog tired, and when the caravan reached the trees, Polk was quick to dismount. He wiped at his sunburned face, and bent over, holding his back and stretching his tired muscles.

It appeared that Jake Polk hadn't been in a saddle for a ride of this duration in a long, long time.

Then Robert Shorter marched up to his brother with his eyes blazing. "Jake, why are we stopping now? We can make another mile or two easy before dark. We have to keep moving, we can't stop now."

Polk had an exasperated, weary look on his face. "Bobby, it's

212

time to stop and rest the horses. You go on back to your books and your drawings. I'll get us to the canyon as fast as we can get there. If I need your help, I'll ask for it. Otherwise keep away from me."

Clint saw that Shorter had been taken aback at the sharp retort. He stared hard at his brother, but returned to his wagon without further comment.

Polk pointed a finger at Clint and said, "Ramsay, you go scrounge up some firewood." Then he shouted at the two women who were climbing off the wagon. "Siena, you and the Holliday woman dig around in the second wagon and come up with some of the grub we loaded and start cooking."

Clint gathered an arm full of dead branches and built a fire in the middle of the camp. While doing so, he noticed that John Henry never took his eyes off either Calico or Siena as they moved around the camp trying to get a meal together.

That man is going to be trouble. And soon.

He kept reminding himself to be patient. The right time would come. He had to be ready when it came.

At sunup, Polk had the camp up and moving. He was shouting out orders to Hocker, Siena, the gunmen, and the mule skinners. Nothing seemed to suit him.

"Getting impatient?" Clint asked.

"Shut your flytrap," Polk said. "I ain't got no time to waste on the niceties of life. I'm going after that gold and nothing's going to stop me."

Even at that, Clint noticed that he backed off somewhat a little later. Polk paced around the campfire while Calico had bacon sizzling in the pan, and coffee boiling on the fire. Clint drank a cup of coffee and tried to plan out his strategy for the day. To his way of thinking, he had to find a way to delay their travel for another day if possible. He had been successful in taking them a little off course toward the west, which, in his mind, would delay their arrival at the canyon by several hours. He now looked at the low hills, the jutting mesas, and tall buttes around him. A thought then occurred to him that Polk might buy.

"Polk," he said. "I'm beginning to recognize some of the landmarks around here now. In fact, I think we might have made a dry camp right where we are now way back in sixty-nine after we left the canyon. If memory serves me right, we hung tight to the foothills leaving the canyon and got here in a day, always keeping them to our right. If we reverse that same route, keep the foothills to our left, it should lead us straight to the canyon by the shortest route."

"You say it took you a day from the pass to here?"

Clint looked to the sky, pretending to think hard about the question. "We were riding hard at the time, and we didn't have any wagons or women to slow us down. So I'm thinking it will take us another day and a half at best with what we have along with us now. But I'm confident this is the place where we camped that night."

He threw in a little flattery for good measure. "You've got us on the right trail."

Shorter was sitting by the fire and heard their conversation. He threw his coffee remains into the fire and said, "Jake, I want to get there tomorrow at the latest."

"I think that's possible," Clint said. "It might be late tomorrow, but if we push our stock hard—and we don't run into a band of renegade Comanche or Kiowa warriors, we can make it sometime tomorrow."

John Henry was standing off to their left saddling his horse, when all of a sudden he drew his gun and pointed it toward the top of a low hill off to the east. "Look, who's that?"

They all looked where he was pointing. On top of the hill

silhouetted by the rising sun was a single rider on a horse. The rider carried a feathered lance and sat watching them.

"Comanches," Shorter said in a frightened voice. "They've spotted us. This was my greatest fear."

"You can't keep them on reservations forever," Clint said. "We tried for years. There's no way to stop them when they get the urge to leave. And where there's one, there's bound to be more."

"Look, over there," Hocker said, pointing to a hill behind them. "Another one."

Tay Redwing came over and joined them. "Do not like Comanche," he said. "Bad enemy."

"You're not scared of them are you, Redwing?" Hocker said.

Redwing's hand dropped to his gun, but he stopped short of pulling. He took a step closer to Hocker, and stood face-to-face with him. "Good to be scared of Comanche."

"I wonder how many of them there are," Shorter said, his voice betraying the fear he felt in his stomach.

"They're scouts," Clint said. "I'd say we'll find out sooner rather than later how many are out there. It's common for twenty or thirty young warriors to band together and escape on raiding parties in order to make a name for themselves. These horses and mules we have will look pretty appetizing to them. Not to mention all these Winchesters."

Clint noticed that Tay Redwing, the Caddo half-breed, took another look at the hills as he walked away from them.

CHAPTER FIFTY-EIGHT

Siena Welborn was worried and scared too. When she saw the Comanche watching them, and then heard the talk about renegade raiding parties, she began to shiver. Never in her wildest imagination had she foreseen herself being in this kind of fix. All her life she had heard tales of brutal atrocities wrought on female captives by Indians.

She ran over to Polk and said, "Jake, we have to go back. I told you I would go anywhere with you, but I never expected anything like this. We can't go on, it's too dangerous. Please, for all our sakes, let's turn back now. All the gold in the world isn't worth risking our lives like this."

"Easy now, Siena," Jake said, as he pulled her back to the covered wagon. "Don't forget about you, me, and New Orleans. We've come this far together. There's no need to turn back now. That's why we brought Redwing and John Henry along. They can handle anything the Comanches can throw at us."

She wanted to believe him, but what she saw on the ridges was more persuasive. "But I'm scared, Jake." She raised a fist and pounded him on the chest. "I want to go back now! I don't care about the gold. I just want to go back." She put her hands to her face and began crying.

She was still talking to him as he turned and walked away. As he did, he looked over at John Henry and jerked a thumb toward her. "She's all yours now, John Henry. I don't have time to listen to all her blubbering. Do what you want with her."

Siena saw the look in the giant's eyes. She had seen him staring at her before and was deathly afraid of him. She backed
away as far as she could, then tripped over the wagon tongue.
She scrambled to her feet and tried to run, but Anse Hocker
caught hold of her arm and shoved her toward John Henry.

"Here, big boy," Hocker said, laughing. "Catch."

Lockhart grabbed her around the waist and slung her over
his shoulder. She screamed and kicked at him, but he just
laughed at her clumsy attempts to get away from him.

"Jake, help me!" she yelled. "Please help me. I didn't mean it.
I'll go with you to get the gold. I'll go with you to New Orleans.
Help me."

John Henry dropped her to the ground in the middle of the
camp. He stood over her with a ruthless scowl on his face.
"Shut up, you little tramp. You heard him. You're mine now."

Robert Shorter pushed his way past Hocker and Polk and
rushed over to where John Henry stood. "Leave her alone, Lockhart. She's as much a part of this outfit as you are now, so back
off. I'm the one who gives orders around here, and I'm telling
you to leave her be."

"Well, hell's bells," Polk said with a grin plastered on his
craggy face. "Is little Bobby Shorter showing some backbone
for once in his life?" He turned to Hocker, who had his hand on
his gun ready to draw, and said, "Look at him, Anse. Bobby
here is acting like he's one tough hombre. And he still thinks
he's the boss. Show him who's boss, John Henry."

John Henry let out a whoop, then hit Shorter across the
mouth with a wicked backhand. The artist, author, and the man
who had dreamed up the whole dirty scheme flew backwards
into the campfire.

Clint ran over and dragged him away from the blaze before
he could be burned.

"Let's see how tough he really is," Lockhart said, pushing

217

Clint aside. He reached down and pulled Shorter up and slapped him again and again with his open hand, then dropped him to the ground. Blood poured from Shorter's mouth. One of his eyes was nearly closed, and his nose had taken on an odd shape. Shorter curled himself into a fetal position and lay still as John Henry kicked at him.

Polk strolled over and stepped between them. "That's enough, John Henry. I think he knows who's in charge now."

John Henry did as he was told, then turned to Siena and said, "You're mine now, little lady. Just you remember that. You're mine."

Siena crossed her arms across her chest and began sobbing.

Jake got behind his brother and helped him to his feet. "From now on, you best keep your mouth shut, Bobby. You've lived a different life than we've lived. You've had the schooling I never had and never wanted. I've come up the hard way, fighting to get everything I could, by any means. I know you don't understand my way, but hear me now. Just because we had the same father don't mean nothing to me. Stay out of our way, or you're going to get hurt real bad. You've pointed us toward this gold, and we aim to get it. If we gotta kill some people in the process, too bad. And, little brother, I'm afraid that includes you. So you go on back to the wagon with your books and paintbrushes and keep your mouth shut. You might stay alive that way."

Shorter wiped at his swollen mouth with a handkerchief, swaying back and forth, trying to remain on his feet. "But, Jake . . . it was my idea . . . my plan . . . part of that gold belongs to me. You're not going to deny me my share, are you?" He looked around at everyone, his eyes pleading: Calico, Siena, Clint.

"They can't help you, Bobby. They'll be lucky if they get out of this alive. Now you go on and get in the wagon like I said. If you don't give us any more trouble, we might change our minds."

Calico helped Siena to her feet and they walked over to the covered wagon together. Calico handed her a white handkerchief. "Here, Siena, use this."

Siena looked at Calico with a crooked smile and said, "Thanks. I kind of made a fool out of myself, didn't I?"

"If it's any consolation, I heartily agree with your sentiments."

"I can't believe Shorter stood up for me like that," Siena said. "No one has ever done anything like that for me before without expecting something in return. Jake just stood there and laughed at me while that giant threw me around. And to think I was ready to go off to New Orleans with that crazy madman. What a damned fool I've been. Now I've got that giant to deal with."

Calico sat back and tried to clear her mind. Too much was happening. She searched around for Clint, but she couldn't find him. She put her hands to her face and said a silent prayer.

Then Polk starting yelling. "Get moving, everybody. Now that we have everything straight between us, we're going after that gold, Comanches or no Comanches. Anybody says different, say it now. We've wasted enough time already."

Calico heard nothing but the faraway howl of a coyote.

CHAPTER FIFTY-NINE

Clint took the point beside Polk as the caravan rolled on. Twice he spotted the two Comanche riders following them at a distance, both well out of rifle range. Once he pointed out three Comanches to Polk.

"Their numbers are growing," Clint said. "I chased them for years when I was in the cavalry and with the Rangers. I got an arrow in my right leg at Frenchman's Creek a few years back for a souvenir. Unless I miss my guess, these are young bucks off the reservation looking to make their mark. They're looking to impress the young squaws back in their tepees. If they can take a few scalps and guns back with them, they'll be considered big men in the tribe."

"Why're they just watching us?" Polk asked. "If they're going to attack, what are they waiting on?"

"Don't forget, it was a renegade Comanche raiding party that attacked those Mexican bandits twelve years ago. They might be waiting for us to be as dumb as those *banditos* and make the same mistake. We could go into the canyon and make their work real easy. They've heard the stories the old men tell. Back then, Wolf Eye led around two dozen young warriors who were desperate for horses and guns. I suspect these warriors are in the same fix now as they were back then. They escaped from the reservation with just the breechclouts they're wearing, and a few weapons they had stolen. They need horses and guns—and we've got 'em."

Polk rode over to talk to Hocker and Redwing. Clint watched as the greedy thieves put their heads together and talked, looking up at the Comanche riders as they did so. John Henry was riding off to the left and seemed to be getting more nervous with each passing minute. His head was never still, always turning, watching. Clint had already begun to sense a growing anxiety among the outlaws. He knew being stalked by Comanche warriors could unnerve the strongest-willed person. He'd been there often, and understood.

Polk returned with a grim expression on his face.

"It's getting chancier by the mile, wouldn't you say, Polk? I've seen the results of one bloodbath in these parts, thanks to the Comanche. I'd hate to see another one. Worse than that, I'd hate to be in one."

"I wouldn't worry too much about the Indians if I were you," Polk said. "You're not going to be around much longer anyway. If the Indians don't kill you, it'll be my pleasure to do the job for them. Right now your job is to get us to that place where the gold is hid. That's the one thing that's kept you and the Hollidays alive so far. I would advise you to make the best of your last few days."

Travel on that second day was slow, much slower than the first day. The stock was tiring and everyone was on edge, watching the hills and ridges for signs of the Comanches, which wasn't too difficult. There was at least one Comanche warrior in view at all times keeping them in sight.

Polk appeared more nervous as they came closer and closer to the canyon. Clint knew Polk was as scared of a Comanche attack as all the others, but his greed was greater than his fear, thus he continued on toward the canyon. As for Robert Shorter, he was now a broken man. He was fearful of his brother and fearful of the Comanches. He lay in the wagon bed, swallowed up in his own self-pity.

As dusk approached, Clint rode to Polk's side. "Polk, I know you're calling the shots now, but I think it would be smart to stop here for the night." Clint pointed to a thick stand of trees at the base of a mesa off to their left. "That's as good a spot to defend as we're going to find. I wouldn't want to be traveling any farther in this light. It would be a perfect time for an attack."

Polk was more than displeased that they had not yet reached the canyon where the gold was hidden. Still, he recognized what Ramsay was saying was true.

To soothe Polk's mind, Clint pointed to the north of where they sat. "See that break in the hills?"

Polk stood in his stirrups and looked in that direction. "Yeah, I see it."

"That's the pass we've been heading for."

"Are you sure?" he said.

"I'm sure." In reality, Clint was sure of only one thing: if an opportunity for him to act didn't come soon, he and the Hollidays were going to be in deep trouble.

CHAPTER SIXTY

The night was clear and cool with a cloudless sky above them. A light breeze wafted through the nooks and crannies of the mesas; a welcome change after the day of stifling heat they had endured. A half-moon cast its light along the desert, creating ghostlike shadows along the jagged mesa walls. Clint sat with Calico and Justus around a small fire, finding little to talk about given their precarious circumstances. Justus seemed to be holding up well. His leg had been causing him some pain as the travel over the uneven terrain had jolted and jarred him unmercifully. Still, he'd handled his difficulty with few complaints. Clint knew the aches and pains in his leg were the least of Justus's worries.

They had sat and stared at the fire for several minutes, when Justus stood and stretched his arms over his head. "I'm going over to the wagon. I'm going to fire up my pipe, and try to forget all this for a while. It might not work, but I'm going to give it a try."

Clint helped him walk to the wagon, then returned to the fire. He sat down beside Calico and said, "Want to have a long talk?"

"You meant *the* long talk?"

He nodded. "Yep, the one we've been putting off. But the talk might not be as long as I intended for it to be."

She looked down at her hands and whispered, "I'm not sure I want to have this talk, Clint. I'm not sure I want to hear what you have to say."

Clint was taken aback by her response. That wasn't the answer he had expected. Had he been misreading the signs all along? He sat there and stared into her blue eyes. He reached out and took her hands in his. "Calico, I need to say what's on my mind. After I finish, then it'll be done and we can move on with our lives."

She nodded her head. "Go on, Clint, say what you have to say. I'll listen."

He took a deep breath and said, "Some time ago I spotted a ranch in the Texas panhandle. A beautiful place, good grass and plenty of water. The old rancher who owns the place told me he was ready to call it quits, since he couldn't keep the place up like he wanted due to his failing health. He offered it to me for a reasonable price."

Clint could see that Calico was becoming more animated as he described the ranch. Her eyes began to glow as he talked on about the place.

"With a little hard work and some luck, a couple of people could turn it into a fine ranch. I have the will to work hard, and I have the money to buy the land. I just need another person who's willing to join me. I had hoped it might be you."

Calico gazed down at the fire and began to stir at the coals. Then she looked up and said, "I need you to answer one question for me."

Clint knew his heart was pounding, and he was scared to hear what she was about to ask.

"One question? Well . . . Sure, I guess I can do that."

She sat up straight, looked him squarely in the eyes and said, "Harley told me there was a girl from your past that you couldn't get out of your mind. Someone you couldn't forget." She hesitated for a few seconds, then continued. "I want to know, and you had better tell me the truth. Will this girl, or this woman, ever cause a problem for us sometime in the future?"

Clint felt his body relax, and he almost laughed out loud. But he maintained his composure and, in a serious tone, he said, "Oh, I'm pretty certain the woman Harley mentioned will be a problem sometime in the future. I know that, because she's already been a problem in more ways than one. She's taken a potshot at me for no reason, she's helped me hide from the law, and she's created havoc at every turn. And I've only known her for a few days. So, yes, I fully expect she'll continue to be a problem in the future as well."

Her eyes widened, and she pointed a finger at her chest. "*Me?* I'm the girl you couldn't get out of your mind after all these years?"

"You're the one, Calico. I have never been able to get the little girl I found in those rocks out of my mind. And I never expected to see the little girl again. But to find that she has become the grown-up, beautiful woman named Calico was a wonderful surprise."

She put her hands to her mouth, then said, "Oh, Clint. Yes, I will go with you anywhere."

A grin spread across his face. "It's settled then. When we get out of this little pickle we're in, it's off to the panhandle for us."

She nodded her head. "Yes, it's off to the panhandle."

Then he turned serious. "Listen to me, now that we've had our long talk. We're going to get out of this difficulty, maybe tonight, or maybe tomorrow. But we're going to get out of it, I assure you. You and your dad just need to follow my lead. I plan to be busy when it happens, so you'll have to look after your father for a while."

"But how? We're their prisoners." She waved her hand at the land surrounding them. "And we have Comanches all around us." She took both his hands in hers and put them to her lips. "Oh, Clint, I'm happy, and I'm scared at the same time. I've been through this before, and I know what can happen. And you do too. You promise to be careful. I don't want anything to come between us and that ranch."

"Trust me, okay? You and your father be ready to run when the time comes. Go hard for that big boulder next to the horses. I'll meet you there when I can."

"But . . . but when?"

"I can't say for sure when. All I can tell you is that we'll know when the time comes. You just be ready."

Anse Hocker was sitting close behind them at his fire, taking long drinks from a whiskey bottle at regular increments. Even at that, Clint could tell that he was alert to everything going on around him. Redwing was with the stock and the mule skinners. John Henry was walking the perimeter, sneaking a glance in Siena's direction at every opportunity. Clint was watching him when a coyote howled in the distance, and the big man dove behind a pile of rocks, his gun pointing at the sound.

Clint walked over to the fire where Hocker sat. "You think Polk is going to let you see any of this gold, Anse? He's already cut out his brother and the banker's wife. Which one of you is next, you or John Henry?"

"Whatever happens, you'll never know. I'll put a bullet in you when we get to the gold—or maybe before." He took another gulp of whiskey. "You remember what I say. I'll put a bullet in you."

"You might get your chance. But I don't think you're man enough to get it done."

Then he heard a horse leaving the camp at a gallop.

Hocker jumped up and grabbed his gun. "Dammit, it's Redwing. He's running away."

Hocker took two quick shots in the direction of the disappearing horse and rider. "That no good . . ."

"Don't you recall what Redwing said earlier? He said

something about how it's good to be scared of the Comanches. I guess he was scared enough to make a run for it."

Clint walked away, leaving Hocker with a frown on his twisted face. But Clint walked away smiling. *The odds have now been reduced by one gunman.*

And then he heard the second howl of a coyote.

CHAPTER SIXTY-ONE

Calico left the fire for the wagon soon after Clint walked away. Her father was standing next to the second wagon, toying with his pipe. She joined him and put her arms around his shoulders. "You never expected to be in the middle of anything like this when you took in a nine-year-old orphan, did you?"

He shook his head. "No, honey, I guess not. We've gone through a lot together in those twelve years, haven't we? We've fought droughts, sandstorms, rustlers, illnesses. You name it, we've fought it, and we survived. And I think we all became stronger because of it. Still, I wouldn't trade those rough-and-tumble years for anything." He stepped back, took her by the hands, and looked at her. "Don't give up yet. I have a feeling Clint has something up his sleeve."

"I think so, too, Dad. He told me to be ready to run if anything happens tonight. I want you to move over into the wagon with me."

She stepped up in the wagon and began laying out a blanket for Justus. Siena sat next to Robert Shorter, trying to comfort him as best she could. Calico moved over to sit next to her.

"All he does is stare at the wagon canvas," Siena said. "He doesn't even blink. I think he's lost his mind, or maybe his will to live. And to think, his own brother did this to him."

"Gold fever can cause people to act different."

Siena nodded. "I know. I got caught up in it, too. We're in a real mess now, aren't we?"

"Yes, I think you could call what we are involved in a real mess, among other things. We have killers all around us, and renegade Indians just over the next hill. Yeah, Siena, we're in a real mess."

Calico smoothed out the blanket and said, "These are greedy, brutal men you've been dealing with. They've got the fever now, and they've got it bad. I doubt if any of us will get out alive, even those men Polk brought along to protect him. If they should find gold in the canyon, I'll wager anything they will end up killing each other before a dime of it is spent. Look how they treated you and Shorter. And you know what Jake Polk did to Marva."

Siena reached under her shirt and pulled out small pistol. "They haven't beat me yet. What you say may be true, but I'll get my licks in before I go down."

Calico could well believe that she would. She reached over and patted her hand. "Good luck, Siena. We might be more alike than either of us knows."

Siena smiled at Calico and turned away.

Justus knocked on the wagon sideboard and said, "Can I come in?"

Calico pulled back the canvas flap and helped him climb in. "Take this spot here. I'll sleep next to you." But down deep she had a premonition that sleep was going to be a rare commodity on this night.

CHAPTER SIXTY-TWO

Clint sat on the ground with his back to one of the wagon wheels. His hat was tipped forward over his eyes. To all appearances, he was dozing. But his mind was alert to the sounds of the night. In particular, he was listening for the third howl of a coyote. He'd already heard two of the howls, and sat motionless waiting for number three.

The camp had settled in for the night. Hocker remained seated by the fire lost in his thoughts, with the empty whiskey bottle still clutched in his hand. John Henry walked the perimeter, jumping at every sound. Jake Polk was wrapped up in his blanket under the second covered wagon with his gun in his hand. Everyone else had scattered to their own places for the night.

Half an hour passed before Clint heard the third mournful coyote call from beyond the area occupied by the mule skinners. He pulled his legs back under his body, ready to react when the time came. He pushed back his hat and looked about the camp. No movement. Good.

All of a sudden, a shrill scream came from the rocks above the camp. At the same time, a painted lance with two feathers at its base landed in the middle of the campfire where Hocker sat, scattering glowing coals and sparks in a wide circle. Another shriek came from the other side of the rocks, then another one from the trees behind them. Gunshots rang out from different directions.

Clint was ready and made a mad dash to the rocks in the midst of the confusion. Unseen, he passed John Henry, who was blasting away at every shadow. Clint dived behind a rock and peered into the camp. He saw Polk roll over and position himself behind a wheel of the wagon, holding his fire. *A cool character,* he thought. There was chaos all around. The Mexican mule skinners started running through the camp, yelling and waving their arms. The horses and mules were stampeding along with them.

More shots were fired.

Clint weaved himself through the boulders and fallen rocks, keeping out of sight of the gunmen. He had to find a weapon. Keeping low, he made his way in the direction where he first heard the gunshots. When he reached the boulder where he had told Calico and Justus to meet him, they were not there. He looked around. They were nowhere to be seen.

Then he heard a sound behind him. He turned and saw Harley walk out from the trees holding a smoking Winchester in his hands. He was naked down to the waist, his body covered in a stinking brown dye of some kind. He had black and vermillion stripes painted on his face and body. His long braided hair had feathers dangling across his shoulders to resemble a Comanche warrior as much as possible.

"When I heard your lousy coyote calls, I realized who the Comanches out there really were," Clint said. "You know, you ought to practice on that howl. It's not very good."

"It got the message across, didn't it? And it ran off one of your gunmen, too."

While they were talking, another quasi-Comanche joined them. Like Harley, he was stripped to the waist and painted. A feather hung from his hair and he carried a lance in his hands but no gun.

"Father Matthew," Clint said, shocked at the sight of the

father standing in front of him. "What in God's good name . . ."

"Don't ask. Where are the Hollidays?"

"That's what I'm trying to find out. I haven't seen either of them." Clint turned to Harley. "Quick, Harley, give me your Colt. I have to go find them."

Harley unbuckled his gun belt and handed it to him. "Be careful, pard."

Anse Hocker was always aware of his surroundings. After the lance had interrupted his whiskey-laden meditation, he hurried toward a pile of rocks in the darkest part of the mesa. He swung his rifle left to right looking for a target, but saw nothing except the dust created by the frightened horses. Then he spotted a movement in the trees off to his right. He fired three shots in rapid succession. There was no return fire. He lowered himself to the ground, listening and watching.

There was no more gunfire coming from the spot where John Henry had positioned himself. He supposed the Comanches had killed him. Too bad. The Comanches had saved him the trouble of doing it himself. What about Polk? Where was he? Hocker realized if he stayed where he was, he would be a dead man sooner or later. His best chance was to slip away before the Comanches spotted him. If he could cling to the rock walls, maybe he could sneak away without being seen.

He crouched low and began creeping along the rock wall, feeling his way along. When he reached the end of the wall, he heard someone call out in the darkness.

"Throw down your gun, Hocker."

Ramsay!

"Those three shots you threw into the trees gave away your position. You're done, so you might as well give it up now."

"It's you again, Ramsay. I always figured it would end up this way. You against me."

"Come on out and face me like a man, not like a cowering weasel hiding in the rocks."

"I'm coming out," Hocker said, the whiskey in him giving him courage. "Then we'll see who's best."

Clint was watchful, unable to see more than a few feet in the dim light of the moon. He heard Hocker before he appeared. The gunman was ten feet from Clint when he went for his gun. Clint was ready and pulled a split second quicker. His shot hit Hocker in the chest and the gunman dropped to his knees, balanced there for a few seconds, then fell forward on his face.

Clint walked over to the fallen man and looked down at him. He felt little sympathy for him and men of his ilk. He died as he had lived, a violent man.

Then his mind turned to his real concern. Where was Calico?

CHAPTER SIXTY-THREE

When the shooting in the camp had stopped, Clint stepped out from behind the rocks. Crouching low and moving from obstacle to obstacle, he was still unsure where Polk and John Henry were. Hocker was dead and Redwing had run, of that he was sure. But the other two he didn't know about. He crept a few yards farther along, then saw a leg sticking out from behind a boulder. He eased over to it and found that the leg belonged to John Henry. His sightless eyes were staring upwards at the sky. To Clint's surprise, seated on a rock a few feet away from the dead giant was Siena Welborn. She held a small pistol in her lap. He started to duck behind a rock, but realized that Siena wasn't going to shoot at him. She just sat there motionless, with wide eyes staring at John Henry's lifeless body.

He walked over and stood in front of her.

She looked up at him with a forlorn expression on her tear-streaked face. "He was no good, Ramsay," she said. "He shouldn't have treated Robert that way. Robert was just taking up for me. Nobody ever took up for me before. I was such a fool for getting involved in this crazy scheme. First it was Myron I betrayed, now all this."

She looked beaten and worn down, but he'd seen her in action before, so Clint wasn't taking anything for granted with her.

"Siena, hand me the gun. It's all over. John Henry can't harm you now."

She looked at Clint, then down at the pistol. She stood and tossed the pistol on Lockhart's still body, then walked back toward the wagons.

Clint watched with mixed feelings as she walked away. She was part and parcel to all the misery that had occurred over the past few days. That she came in at the end of Polk's grand scheme might be a mitigating factor, but she'd gotten caught up in the greed and selfishness just like the rest of them. For that, Clint would hold her accountable. But he also believed that all the turmoil she had experienced, and all the hurt she had caused, might have made a lasting impression on her.

Clint went over to John Henry's body and stripped off his gun belt. He checked the cylinder on the big man's gun. Two cartridges. He shucked a handful from John Henry's belt and filled the cylinder. He then hurried over to the wagons where the others had congregated. Wolf Eye and Rosita had joined Harley and Father Matthew. Father Matthew was kneeling down, cleaning Justus's face with a wet cloth. He was alert, but dizzy.

Jake Polk was not with them.

"Where's Calico?" Justus asked. "Did you find her?"

"I was hoping you knew. She didn't show up at the boulder like I asked her to."

"She not here," Rosita said. "I have searched. And the man, Polk, is not here."

Justus lifted himself to his elbows and said, "I climbed out of the wagon right behind Calico. She told me to follow her to that big boulder like you said. When my feet hit the ground, someone hit me and knocked me out. Everything was over by the time I regained my senses." He reached up and grabbed Clint's arm. "Find her, Clint. You have to find her."

So Polk got away—and had taken Calico with him. The burning consolation in Clint's mind was that Polk needed her to get at the gold. With his obsession driving him, Polk wouldn't harm her until she had led him to the spot where Clint had found her years ago.

At least that was the thought he held to in the darkness of the camp.

But another, more troubling, thought surfaced as well. Knowing that Calico was a headstrong, stubborn, independent-minded hellion, she might just buck up to Polk and provoke him into harming her.

Clint walked over to the side of the wagon and stood by himself. He looked at the people who had just risked their own lives to save his and the Hollidays' lives. Wolf Eye and Rosita appeared tired, but rejuvenated by the action. Rosita could have been mistaken for one of Wolf Eye's warriors of old. She played her roll well. Then there was Father Matthew and Harley, who were still hovering over Justus. And Elizano, who was caring for the mule skinners.

Clint went over to Wolf Eye and held out his hand. *"Gracias,"* he said. Then to Rosita, he said, with a slight bow of the head, *"Gracias,* Rosita."

While they were at the wagon talking, Elizano brought the mule skinners to the wagon. They were grinning from ear to ear. "They say they make good Comanches," Elizano said.

Clint learned that the older Mexican had slipped into the camp earlier that evening and had told the three mule skinners what they had planned, and had asked for their help. The mule skinners hadn't been treated well by the *gringos* and were eager to assist. Elizano walked over to stand by Wolf Eye and Rosita. He bent and gave his daughter a kiss on both cheeks.

Clint held out his hand to the old Mexican. *"Gracias,* for now, and for twelve years ago."

Elizano bowed his head. "Find Little One again, *senor.* "

Clint surveyed the wrecked campsite. He would let them

decide whether to remain at the camp overnight, or put a few miles behind them. Sleep, he guessed, would be a long time coming after the excitement of this night. Clint joined Harley and Father Matthew near the wagon and said, "Harley, you and Father Matthew get things organized here and head back to the ranch with everyone whenever you think the time is right. Turn Shorter and Siena over to Sheriff Elder and let him deal with them as best he can."

"And you?" Harley asked.

"I'm going after Calico."

"I thought as much. I got you the best horse in the bunch, saddled and ready to ride."

Clint returned Harley's belt and gun to him, then strapped on the gun belt he had taken off John Henry. He scavenged the camp and came up with two Winchesters to go along with John Henry's Colt. While he was doing that, Harley found a sack and filled it with jerky and hardtack and a few cans of dried fruit. Rosita rounded up two canteens which she filled from one of the wagon's water barrels.

"Here, take this. It might come in handy," Harley said, as he handed Clint his spyglass.

"Thanks, it might at that."

Clint was not anxious to be traveling at night, but there was no other option. Besides, he was certain that Polk hadn't given up on getting his hands on the gold. He hoped and prayed he could get to the canyon ahead of him.

When he was ready to ride, Wolf Eye appeared at his side on his horse and holding a rifle. "I go with you. I know short way."

Clint looked at the old warrior and knew he couldn't refuse the offer.

"Let's go," he said. "I'll follow you."

Clint turned and nodded at Harley, who was scratching his

beard in wonderment as he watched the two old enemies ride away toward Massacre Canyon with a common purpose in mind.

CHAPTER SIXTY-FOUR

Clint and Wolf Eye made no effort to find Polk's trail in the dark. To Clint's way of thinking there was no need to waste precious time with slow, methodical tracking. Polk would head straight for the canyon, of that he was certain. Wolf Eye had taken the lead as they left the camp. But instead of sticking close to the foothills and skirting them as most men would have done, Wolf Eye steered them through a maze of narrow, twisting openings among the ancient landslides and fallen rocks. The old warrior changed directions often, and their travel had slowed due to the unstable terrain. Clint became concerned about their deliberate pace, but he continued to follow the Comanche without questioning the old warrior's judgment.

Knowing that Calico was out there somewhere with Jake Polk drove him onward.

As dawn appeared, Wolf Eye halted at the base of a steep rock wall and pointed at an almost invisible narrow break in the steep rocky walls. "Canyon," he said. "You stay." Wolf Eye then disappeared through the narrow opening.

Clint waited for an agonizing half hour, or longer, before Wolf Eye returned.

"Polk man not here," Wolf Eye said. "We go."

Clint followed Wolf Eye through the narrow opening and realized they had come into the canyon several hundred yards from where he had entered with the cavalry twelve years ago. He turned in the saddle and had difficulty finding the opening they had just ridden through. As they rode farther into the canyon, Clint had no trouble recognizing it as the location of the bloody massacre. There were still remnants of the old pack train scattered along the canyon floor: broken wheel spokes, rotting barrel staves, and a few pieces of charred wagon beds. Still, the canyon looked much different than it had looked the first time he'd seen it. This time around there were no scalped bodies, or black vultures to be seen.

Wolf Eye showed no sign that he'd ever been there.

They rode on for another ten minutes when Wolf Eye held up his right hand. "There," he said, pointing toward a spot high in the rocks. "The cave where I left Elizano and Little One."

Clint looked to where he was pointing but could see nothing but rocks, boulders, and thick brush. The cave, like the narrow opening they had used to enter the canyon, was well concealed from sight. Clint now understood why the cave had not been found by the many treasure seekers who had flocked to the canyon searching for the gold. Its location was well-hidden and known only to the Comanches.

"Is that where Elizano hid the gold?" Clint asked.

"Elizano buried yellow rocks in cave. Hard to find."

But the gold had never been Clint's objective. It was not important to him. It was Calico he wanted. He'd put all his eggs into this one basket, this one decision: that Jake Polk would bring Calico to the canyon. Polk had no way of knowing who the Comanches who'd attacked the camp really were. Clint was holding on to the thought that Polk believed everyone at the camp had all been killed, leaving him alone to find the gold.

Clint didn't want to think about the consequences of him being wrong. With that decision made, the problem he now faced was how to go about rescuing Calico from Polk without her being hurt in the process.

CHAPTER SIXTY-FIVE

Clint quizzed Wolf Eye as to the best way to proceed. Clint had chased the Comanche warrior for years and had always been outsmarted by his cunning, and clever maneuvering. Never would he have imagined that one day he would be soliciting the old warrior's opinion.

While they talked, Clint had kept his eyes and ears alert for any sign of Polk and Calico. Polk had Robert Shorter's map showing him the route to the canyon. Clint remembered from seeing the map that the route he would take would bring them to the northern entrance, the same entrance the cavalry had used twelve years ago. That was where he expected Polk to show.

With time running out on them, Clint and Wolf Eye decided on a plan. Clint wasn't sure it was a good plan, but it would probably work. Wolf Eye's simple solution was to wait in the rocks and shoot Polk when he entered the canyon. One shot and it would be finished. Clint liked the plan, except for Calico being with Polk. He was determined not to do anything that would put her in danger—put her in the line of fire.

So he rejected Wolf Eye's plan and came up with an alternate one. Clint knew it was a risky plan from the start. The key would be Wolf Eye. Could the old warrior pull it off?

Wolf Eye took their two horses and disappeared with them. Ten minutes later he reappeared carrying his rifle and a hunting knife, which was stuck in his leather belt. "We go," he said.

"Polk man and Little One not far."

Clint jerked his head toward the entrance. *How would he know that?*

Clint followed Wolf Eye up the steep rocky terrain.

Wolf Eye pointed to the right and said, "Good place. Go."

Clint took that to mean that was where he should lie in wait. Wolf Eye continued on and melted into the rocks a few yards farther up the climb. Clint still had no clear idea of where the cave was located. The position Wolf Eye had suggested he take was in the midst of a rocky enclave, located to the right and below the spot where Wolf Eye had vanished.

Clint waited and watched. Time crept by. Clint thought about what Wolf Eye had earlier told him about the cave. The Comanche people of generations past had known of the cave, which was concealed from the canyon floor. Warriors of old had made use of it as circumstances had warranted. Tradition among the Comanche people had called for discretion in its use. In Clint's mind, he concluded that the cave had been used only in emergency situations. The Comanche people hadn't wanted their enemies to know of its existence. Wolf Eye said he'd used it two times to escape from his enemies. The last time he had used the cave was for Elizano and Little One over twelve years ago. Others might have used it since. Wolf Eye said he didn't know.

After an hour, he heard a low whistle coming from Wolf Eye's position. Clint pulled out Harley's spyglass and swept the area, left to right, then back again. His heart jumped as he saw Polk and Calico enter the canyon riding on a single horse. Calico in front, Polk behind her.

Wolf Eye's plan would have put her in the line of fire.

He could see that she was riding tall and straight, even under these terrible conditions. He could also see that her hands were tied in front of her, and that Jake Polk had a gun in his hand, stuck in Calico's back.

He continued to watch their every move. The two of them talked for a minute, then Clint saw Calico slowly turn her head from side to side.

She's looking for the spot where I found her.

He watched as she lifted her bound hands and pointed them at a spot far in front of her. The outcropping. She had found it! *That's it, Calico.*

Polk spurred the horse and rode over to the spot Calico had pointed out. He dismounted, looked around, and then pulled Calico off the horse. She looked up the steep incline toward where the cave could be found. She nodded toward it and said something to Polk. He reached into a saddlebag and retrieved a leather sack and slung it over his shoulder. He then pushed Calico forward toward the rocks, his gun still pointed at her back.

When they reached the rocks, she stopped and turned around. She held out her hands and said something to Polk. Polk said something back to her, and held the gun up to her face, then took out a knife and sliced through the rawhide binding and freed her hands.

Good girl.

Clint held his breath as Polk and Calico began trudging up the rocky slope. His first wish was that Polk would separate himself from Calico far enough to give him a clear, clean rifle shot. But he didn't want to take that chance unless there was no other option. If he missed, Polk could use Calico as a shield, or a hostage. Or even worse, his shot might hit her either straight on, or with a ricochet.

He continued to watch as Calico and Polk stopped on the slope. Calico pointed toward a spot to her left, close to where Wolf Eye was hidden. The two of them turned and trudged up the hill in that direction, fighting through the thick brush and thorny scrub. Polk walked behind Calico as she blazed the trail. When they came to the spot where she had pointed, she said something that Clint could not make out. But Polk pushed her aside and began pulling at brush. Some of the brush was thick-rooted and difficult to tear out. Clint watched as the outlaw tore away enough brush to peep through a small opening, but it was much too narrow for him to pass through.

Polk took out his skinning knife and began chopping feverishly at the brush.

Clint could tell that he was wearing down as he tugged at the deep-rooted plants. Then to his surprise, he heard Polk shouting. Clint twisted his head to get a better listening angle.

"The cave!" Polk shouted, while dancing around like a medicine-show shill. "Bobby was right! He was right!" He returned to his chopping with renewed vigor.

Clint turned the spyglass toward Calico, who was standing near Polk and watching him. Then Polk reached over and grabbed her by the shoulders and shoved her to the ground. He took rawhide strips from his pocket and again tied her hands and feet. Polk then rolled her over to the edge of the brush he had removed from the cave opening.

Clint jerked his rifle up and prepared to shoot as soon as he stood. But Polk didn't stand. He remained bent over as he pulled and chopped at the roots of the brush. Clint was getting restless watching Polk. He was further incensed when he saw Polk throw Calico to the ground. But he didn't have that clean, clear shot he so desperately needed.

After several minutes, Polk had a fashioned a hole large enough for him to crawl through. Clint watched as he picked up the leather sack lying at his feet and pulled himself through the opening. Once inside, he broke off more of the brush and widened the opening enough for him to go in and out unobstructed. He left Calico lying outside the cave entrance by the brush.

"Now, Wolf Eye," Clint whispered to himself. "Now, before Polk pulls her inside." A helpless feeling washed over him. There she was, lying there, bound hand and foot with rawhide strips, and there was nothing he could do about it. All he could do was watch the little drama play out from his concealed position. He held his breath. Then he spotted movement behind Calico. Wolf Eye had crawled into his view to within a few feet of Calico. Wolf Eye reached out with his knife and sliced through her bonds.

She jerked her head around, and Clint saw Wolf Eye give her the shush sign. She looked back at the cave opening, then both of them backed away into the thick brush and disappeared from sight.

CHAPTER SIXTY-SIX

A few minutes later, Clint was relieved beyond words when he looked down at the canyon floor and saw Wolf Eye and Calico winding their way through the rocks to safety. Now it was him and Jake Polk. Just the two of them. He repositioned himself in his little rocky fortress and put his hands around his mouth.

"Hey, Polk," he shouted. "Do you want to give yourself up?"

There was a long silence. Clint wasn't sure Polk had heard him, so he repeated his offer.

"So you managed to get away from the Comanches, did you?" Polk shouted back. "I've got the gold, Ramsay. It's here, just like Bobby said. And I've got your little gal, too. You wouldn't want her caught in the middle of a gunfight would you?"

"Take a quick look outside, Jake. I won't shoot. Go ahead. Take a look."

Clint saw the brush that was left standing in the opening move slightly. Polk had looked out of the opening.

Clint shouted at Polk again. "You got all caught up with gold fever, Polk, and lost your one hope of getting away. Calico is already on her way back to her ranch by now. It's just you and me. Oh, by the way, Anse Hocker thought he was a better man than me and found out he was mistaken. Do you want to make that same mistake?"

While he was talking, Clint spotted a rifle barrel poking out of the cave opening. He pulled up his Winchester and fired two quick shots around the barrel's location.

"Gonna have to shoot better than that, Ramsay. Listen to me. There's enough gold in here for all of us. How about it?"

"No thanks. You see, I've got time on my side. You can't stay in there forever. Those small hot caves in this country make a man mighty thirsty. You shouldn't last too long in this heat. I watched you go up the slope to the cave. I didn't see any canteens. All I've got to do is wait here for a few hours, maybe even a day if necessary, but in the end, all the gold will be mine. What do you think about them apples?"

Clint saw movement around the brush again. He trained his rifle on the spot, ready to pull the trigger. But Polk never gave him an opening. Instead, Polk shouted out again, "What kind of deal are you offering if I come out?"

"No deals. Throw out your gun and come out with your hands where I can see them."

"We can split the gold right down the middle. How about it? It's got to be more than a detective can make in a lifetime. Don't that sound good?"

"You heard me. No deals."

As soon as he answered, Clint saw a brown object whirling in his direction. Was it Polk's gun? Was he giving up? Then he recognized the object for what it was. A stick of dynamite! Clint threw himself to the ground and buried his face into the rocky soil. The explosion came seconds later. Dirt, rocks, and debris covered him from head to toe. To his relief, the dynamite hadn't been thrown far enough. Clint now knew why Polk had engaged him in a shouting match. He was trying to judge the distance to his location.

Clint raised his head and looked at the cave opening. If Polk had one stick of dynamite in that leather sack, he could have more. He moved to his left, to position himself more in front of the cave where he had a better view of the opening and away from his rocky enclave. This time he wouldn't give Polk the opportunity to learn where he was located. He sat there and waited for the outlaw to make the next move.

"Hey, Ramsay, you still out there?"

Silence.

"How about it, Ramsay, want to make a deal now?"

Clint had a sudden thought. He scampered back to his original location in the stone enclave and answered. "Sure, Jake, I'll make a deal. Throw down your guns and come on out. It'll take more than one stick of dynamite to get me. I'm snugged down here in a stone fortress."

He then hurried back to the other position in front of the cave and waited. He had his rifle cradled on a rock and ready for what was to come. It wasn't long before he saw the brush move. A few seconds later, Polk showed himself at the cave entrance with a bundle of dynamite in his hand. The fuse was sparking. Just as Polk drew back his arm to throw the dynamite at the stone fortress, Clint fired.

The bullet hit Polk in the shoulder causing him to drop the dynamite at his feet. Clint watched as Polk scrambled after the explosives, scratching at the dirt floor in a futile effort to get to the bundle. But it remained just out of reach.

"No, no!" Polk screamed. "Ramsay, help me, help me! I've got the gold! I'm rich, help me!"

Clint could hear Polk's frantic screams, but knew there was nothing he could do to help him now. He ducked down behind a huge boulder a few seconds before a massive explosion, much larger and louder than the first one, shook the canyon walls. A landslide of rocks and boulders from far above the cave came rushing down, creating an enormous dust cloud over the whole area. Clint lay on his stomach with his head buried in his arms as rocks, dust, and brush fell all around him.

When the air had cleared, he raised his head and saw that the cave that had once been the source of their misery, and the enormous cliff above it, had disappeared. And Jake Polk and his gold had disappeared with it. All that was left was an immense pile of broken rocks.

Jake Polk had gotten in death what he had wanted all his life; he was a man surrounded by gold.

CHAPTER SIXTY-SEVEN

Clint got to his feet and wiped the dust and grime from his face
and eyes. He gave the rock slide one last glance, then walked
toward the canyon floor, thinking: it's finished. Calico ran up
the slope to meet him and threw her arms around his neck. She
hugged him and kissed him, and he could see relief written all
over her face.

"Those explosions—are you all right? Are you hurt?" she
asked.

"I'm fine," he said, looking into her deep blue eyes. "It's all
over now, Calico, all over."

She took both his hands in hers and looked at him. "There
was one memory that kept me sane all the time I was with Jake
Polk. I kept repeating it over and over in my mind. It was
something you said to me twelve years ago." She pointed to a
spot a few feet from where they stood. "It was right there where
you held out your arms to me and said, *I'll not let anyone hurt
you. You're safe now, sweetheart. I promise, I'll not let anything happen to you.* You kept that promise again."

"I remember," he said. "And how about the other memories
tied to this canyon. Those memories both of us have tried hard
to forget."

"Oh, I so dreaded coming back here," she said. "I shivered at
the thought. I was so scared of what might happen. But when I
rode into the canyon, the sight of the rotting wagon beds, broken
wheels, and even the white bones of the mules did not affect me
at all. It was just a calm, sandy place with a few odds and ends

of junk lying around. It's not that much different than the gully behind our ranch where we toss our old junk. So I'm glad to know that I can now put everything about this awful place behind me."

"We can both put it behind us."

A few minutes later, Wolf Eye came forward leading three horses. He pointed to where the cave of his people once was. "Gold back in ground where it belongs. Cause no more trouble." He turned, mounted his horse, and rode away toward the camp where Rosita and Elizano would be waiting for him.

"Calico, you know we can never tell anyone about this location," Clint said. "Some enterprising engineer would figure out how to get to that gold. This has to be our little secret. Do you agree?"

She nodded. "Yes, our secret, forever."

She then turned and watched as Wolf Eye rode out of Massacre Canyon. "For all his misdeeds, Wolf Eye has been there for me more than once. And so have you."

"Who's keeping score?"

Calico smiled and said, "Me. I'm keeping score. And the way I figure it, I now owe you two. Number one was twelve years ago, right here at this canyon. Number two was keeping John Henry away from me on the trail. This time goes down as number three. My single score was holding off John Henry and Redwing at Gimpy's cave. So, Mister Ramsay, you're going to have to put up with me at that panhandle ranch until I can repay you in full."

"Just out of curiosity, how do you plan to pay this debt?"

She threw her arms around him and kissed him again, and again. "This will be the down payment, until we can find a way to finalize the deal."

"Hmmm," he said. "I think I'm going to like you being in debt to me."

ABOUT THE AUTHOR

Ben Tyler is a graduate of Murray State University with a degree in secondary education. He is a former schoolteacher and a former human resources manager in the chemical manufacturing industry. When he is not seated in front of his laptop, the author might be found hacking his way around the local golf course. He currently lives in Western Kentucky near Kentucky Lake.